LORD OF THE MASQUERADE

ROGUES TO RICHES #7

ERICA RIDLEY

COPYRIGHT

Copyright © 2021 Erica Ridley
Cover Design © Erin Dameron-Hill

This is a work of fiction. Names, characters, places, and incidents are the product of the author's imagination or are used fictitiously. Any resemblance to actual events, locales, or persons, living or dead, is purely coincidental.

All rights reserved. Except as permitted under the U.S. Copyright Act of 1976, no part of this publication may be reproduced, distributed, or transmitted in any form or by any means, or stored in a database or retrieval system, without the prior written permission of the author.

ALSO BY ERICA RIDLEY

The *Dukes of War*:
The Viscount's Tempting Minx
The Earl's Defiant Wallflower
The Captain's Bluestocking Mistress
The Major's Faux Fiancée
The Brigadier's Runaway Bride
The Pirate's Tempting Stowaway
The Duke's Accidental Wife

The *Wild Wynchesters*:
The Governess Gambit
The Duke Heist
The Rake Mistake
The Perks of Loving a Wallflower

***Rogues to Riches*:**
Lord of Chance
Lord of Pleasure
Lord of Night
Lord of Temptation
Lord of Secrets
Lord of Vice
Lord of the Masquerade

The *12 Dukes of Christmas*:
Once Upon a Duke
Kiss of a Duke
Wish Upon a Duke
Never Say Duke
Dukes, Actually
The Duke's Bride
The Duke's Embrace
The Duke's Desire
Dawn With a Duke
One Night With a Duke
Ten Days With a Duke
Forever Your Duke

Gothic Love Stories:
Too Wicked to Kiss
Too Sinful to Deny
Too Tempting to Resist
Too Wanton to Wed
Too Brazen to Bite

Magic & Mayhem:
Kissed by Magic
Must Love Magic
Smitten by Magic

The *Wicked Dukes Club*:
One Night for Seduction by Erica Ridley

One Night of Surrender by Darcy Burke

One Night of Passion by Erica Ridley

One Night of Scandal by Darcy Burke

One Night to Remember by Erica Ridley

One Night of Temptation by Darcy Burke

LORD OF THE MASQUERADE

ROGUES TO RICHES #7

ACKNOWLEDGMENTS

As always, I could not have written this book without the invaluable support of my editors and beta crew, with special thanks to Erica Monroe. You are the best!

I also want to thank my wonderful VIP readers, our Historical Romance Book Club on Facebook, and my fabulous early reader team. Your enthusiasm makes the romance happen.

Thank you so much!

CHAPTER 1

London, 1819

*J*ulian Newcombe-Ives, the sixth Duke of Lambley, stood with his hands on the railing of the first-floor promenade encircling the grand ballroom and gazed down on his kingdom. The golden flecks in his hazel eyes glittered in the sparkling light of six crystal chandeliers. The barest hint of a smile teased briefly at his lips.

Everything was exactly as he'd planned it. As he wanted it. As he demanded. He controlled every detail of his weekly masquerades with the same ruthless precision he managed the rest of his dukedom.

Losing control? That was for people like his guests, who were currently engaged in all manner of debauchery and bacchanalia.

Discreet footmen with silver trays moved between the generous champagne towers. Strategically placed refreshment tables were heaped with sweet chocolate, succulent fruits, and other aphrodisiacs.

The orchestra was the finest in London, though only half of Julian's guests had joined the dance floor to waltz with a stranger, their bodies pressed together far closer than was proper.

The other half of his guests were... elsewhere.

Up here, on the first floor, in one of the many sumptuous guest chambers designed for private pleasures. Out on the exterior balconies, seeking the heat of each other's embrace between elegant Chinese folding screens erected to give lovers a semblance of privacy.

Or down in the wild garden below, enjoying the heady scent of spring roses and the anonymity of an inky black sky dotted with stars but devoid of the moon.

The ball opened at ten and ended just before dawn. Masks were worn the entire time—unless, like Julian, one did not care who glimpsed his face. It was his party. He was proud of the elegant hedonism and subversive equality he offered.

Some of the men and women below were lords and ladies. Others were opera singers, barristers, modistes, auctioneers, gamblers. If they were to notice each other at all outside of these walls, it would be to commission a gown or waistcoat, or perhaps only to turn up one's nose and carry on.

But here—*here!* There were no such airs at the Duke of Lambley's masquerades. He did not permit it. Everyone walked through the door to exactly the same reception. In fact—

The door to the exterior receiving room swung open. A pair of ladies with extravagant Venetian masks and barely-there bodices burst inside the grand ballroom.

"Presenting... Lady X, and her companion, Lady X!" the night butler's voice boomed out.

The whirling revelers erupted in cheers, lifting their champagne flutes to cries of, "Lady X! Lady X!"

All of the masquerade guests were Lord or Lady X. Enquiring further was strictly prohibited. Only Julian and his trusted night butler knew their true identities.

Aspiring revelers were welcomed into the receiving room one carriage at a time. First-time guests were required to present a personal invitation, signed and sealed by the duke himself. Their details were then logged in cipher in the night butler's secret ledger, and the invitation destroyed. Guests were then free to entertain themselves however they liked.

The two who had just entered the ballroom looked like any number of other fashionable ladies in extravagant gowns and even more expensive masks. It was impossible to guess their age behind the contours of the porcelain masks and the distraction of colorful feathers and plentiful décolletage on display. Most guests would assume the newcomers were in search of a night's romance with one of the many equally handsome gentlemen in attendance.

Julian happened to know that these two ladies already had their partners in mind. In fact, they'd arrived together. They had eyes for no one but each other. They could not flirt publicly before the pinch-faced patronesses of Almack's or beneath the bright sun at Hyde Park, but here in Julian's domain, they were free to love as they pleased. He allowed himself a small smile of satisfaction.

At the Duke of Lambley's masquerades, society was under *his* control, not the other way around. The only rules were the ones he imposed: Complete anonymity and freedom of choice at every moment.

He had thrown his first such ball a decade ago. A much smaller affair, but the potential was clear from the very first hour. What had begun as a once-a-season indulgence quickly became monthly, then fortnightly, then weekly. During the parliamentary season, his balls were as much an institution as Almack's—and just as exclusive.

For the five months of the social season, the patronesses presided over their insipid assembly rooms every Wednesday evening, and the duke ruled over decadent Saturday nights.

He peered over the enormous ballroom, his eyes missing no detail. Every candle in every chandelier was lit. Every glass of champagne, full. Every refreshment table, overflowing. There were no queues for food or drink. There was an excess of options at every turn, and an army of footmen trained to respond to the slightest cue.

"Presenting Lord X!" the night butler called out.

"Lord X!" roared the crowd with delight.

Julian's servants might not know the names of the men and women they attended, but many of the guests wore the same masks to every masquerade. Hera had staked her claim on Zeus, and so on, leaving nothing to chance so the nameless lovers could be reunited.

Other guests, like Julian, did not pick the same partner twice. Some might be fooled by a change in costume, but not him. He did not forget a face—or even part of a face. He could recognize this lord by the cleft in his chin, or that lady by the sway of her hip.

Julian observed, and he remembered. It was part of what made his parties so memorable. The footmen knew the swan preferred her ratafia slightly less sweet but with extra grapes. They knew the tastes of the gentleman in the crimson mask, the lady with the lavender wig, the highwayman in the domino with its flowing black cape.

Lambley's staff brought each guest exactly what they wanted before the thought even fully formed in their minds. To step into this ballroom was to have one's innermost dreams brought to life.

After committing every current detail to memory, the duke released the banister of the six-foot wide promenade encircling the ballroom and made his way to the marble steps.

The head footman met him on the stairway.

Julian murmured instructions. His staff was used to these constant improvements. If it was possible to perfect the art of the masquerade, Julian intended to achieve it.

A dancer with tired feet? A plush chair, comfortable slippers. Too hot? A footman to relieve milord of his coat or cravat. Too cold? A shawl for madame's shoulders and a pearl pin to keep it closed. No need to return the brooch. A token of the masquerade, compliments of His Grace.

"Presenting Lady X!" called the night butler.

"Lady X!" shouted the crowd, lifting their glasses.

This Lady X was the ballet dancer determined to become the duke's long-term mistress.

Julian did not have a long-term anything, other than his dukedom. Not even his cherished masquerades. Someday soon he would need to take a bride, and that would be more than enough disruption to his schedule, thank you very much.

He could have hurried down the stairs and out of sight before Zylphia glimpsed him, but Julian did not hide from anyone or anything.

She bounded up to him, breathless. "I missed you."

"Good evening, Lady X."

She giggled. "You know it's me."

"And you know the rules," he reminded her. "Anonymity. Freedom of choice. If you are determined to break either of them, your invitation will be rescinded."

"I can understand not wishing to bed the others a second time..." She trailed her fingers up his lapel. "But with me..."

"You should find someone less busy." He removed her hand from his chest. "I've a party to attend to."

She twisted her lips. "I would ask if you ever relax, but we both know the answer to that."

He frowned at the edge to her words. Of course he *relaxed.* He'd spent forty minutes with her in one of the upstairs chambers last month. If that wasn't taking a respite, what was? Normally he did not allow himself a minute over half an hour. Not when there were guests to be looked after. He had been positively negligent.

"I have responsibilities," he reminded her.

She pouted. "And no heart. I pity the woman you take as your wife."

So did Julian, frankly. It was one of the many reasons he had not yet acquired one.

It was not that he didn't believe in the concept of love. He believed in it very much, and created a magical midnight world specifically to bring a sense of romance into the lives of others.

It was the duke himself who was incapable of emotion.

He was exactly as coldhearted as Zylphia accused. He did not *want* to see her again, naked or otherwise. He did not want a mistress. He did not want to confront the same face again, day in and day out. And he definitely did not want to become *close*. Love was for those who could not control their hearts.

There was nothing Julian could not control.

He arched a brow. "If your situation is such that you must acquire a wealthy patron posthaste, three different guests tonight have authorized me to point interested parties in their direction."

She brightened. "Who? Where?"

"Do you see the mask with the hooked nose and the emerald feathers?"

Within minutes, she fluttered off toward a strapping young man whose family had made a respectable fortune on horseflesh. What he and Miss Zylphia arranged outside of this ballroom had no bearing on Julian. He wished them both luck.

He was no rake. Not in the ordinary sense. He did not set out to seduce or to romance. Women were attracted to his power, not his poetic words. This suited him very well. Neither party wishing for more than each was willing to give.

Julian certainly didn't lack for more. What would he wish for? He had everything. The highest title, short of royalty. Enough gold, he might as well *be* royalty. A grand London residence, several country estates, the most well-run households in all of England.

He had not just designed the perfect life, he was *living* it. The last thing he wanted was for it to change.

"Lambley," came a warm male voice.

The duke turned to see the masked Earl and Countess of Wainwright, who had met at one of his masquerades two seasons prior.

He bowed. "Lady X. Lord X."

"You've outdone yourself once again," said the earl.

"I believe you said that last week," Julian murmured.

"It's true every time," the earl replied. "I've no idea how one could possibly improve on perfection, but you astonish me every week without fail."

"I thought *I* astonished you," teased his wife.

The earl scooped her into his arms. "I'm about to astonish *you*," he growled, and carried his bride up the marble stairs without remembering to take his leave from the duke.

Julian grinned. This was what his masquerades were *for*. To enable those capable of love to find it, often in the hearts of the person they least expected, just like the earl and his countess had done.

How horrified they had been when they first discovered the identity of their nameless lover!

And how besotted they were now. An heir at home in the nursery, and his parents as wildly in love as ever.

Julian made his way through the crowd, exchanging pleasantries, accepting compliments, pointing those who wanted something in the direction of that which they desired.

It took half an hour to cross from the rear staircase to the door leading to the receiving vestibule. A record. It often took much longer. His parties were beginning to run themselves.

A footman rushed forward to open the door.

Julian exited the ballroom and stepped into the relative quiet of the receiving room. When the door closed behind him, the buzz of a hundred hushed conversations and the footfalls of the dancers were no longer audible. Only the muffled music from the orchestra slipped through the cracks around the door like the scented smoke of exotic incense.

The night butler grinned at him. "Lambley."

"Fairfax," the duke returned. "Anything to report?"

"All is calm and as you predicted."

Exactly how Julian liked it.

Fairfax handed over the masquerade log for Julian's perusal.

Anthony Fairfax had been Julian's friend long before he became the night butler. As a member of the ton, he recognized the members of the beau monde on sight—and as a former degenerate gambler, Fairfax was well versed in the underworld as well, making him uniquely suited to match faces to invitations.

Anthony Fairfax had been a common sight amongst the beau monde until his family's debts drove him out of the ballrooms and into the gaming hells.

It had not gone well for him at the tables, until the day his new wife won him at a game of cards. And then it had gone worse. Fairfax did not have enough blunt to manage his own matters, much less take on another dependent. That he married "beneath" him only distanced him further from the bon ton.

And then Julian had offered him employment. The money Fairfax needed, at the cost of severing his remaining ties with polite society. A proper gentleman was not *employed*, for God's sake. And definitely not as a night butler at Mayfair's most scandalous masquerades. A veritable *servant*. What a fall from grace!

In truth, Fairfax's position had risen. He controlled access to the most exclusive balls in London. He knew the identities of the masked lords and ladies, checking their blushing faces against the coded register of permitted guests before determining who would be allowed inside and who would not. Fairfax enjoyed more popularity now with certain sets than he ever had as an impoverished, but respectable, gentleman. And infinitely more power.

Julian could certainly understand the allure of that.

And, he admitted, it was rather heady to know who was who, and doing what with whom. It was one of the ways Julian maintained control over his surroundings. By giving people what they desire, predicting the outcome of that action became easy. He much preferred being the grantor of wishes than the victim of whims. Impulsiveness was for fools.

He handed the log back to Fairfax.

"It's a new year," Julian said. "You haven't asked me to augment your salary."

"You raised it last year," Fairfax reminded him. "If I tossed out a number, you're likely to double it."

"It's a paid post, not a game of whist," Julian said. "If I have the blunt to lose, why not take it from me?"

"Because you're my friend."

"Exactly why I want to give it to you. What is money for, if not to be used?"

"With that attitude, I have no idea how you still possess any," Fairfax said. "Wait until you have a wife."

Julian cocked a brow. "She'll spend all of my money?"

"She'll lock you in the attic so that *you* stop spending it," Fairfax replied.

"Then I shall never marry," Julian answered. "I should allow no man or woman to have control over me or my actions."

"Mm-hm." Fairfax smirked. "Remember this conversation after you fall in love."

Julian let out a sigh. "I am incapable of love. Sometimes I wish that were not true."

"Be careful what you say at a masquerade," Fairfax warned. "On nights such as these, even the most unlikely wishes might come true."

Julian cuffed his friend's shoulder and let himself back into the ballroom.

Such words painted a pretty picture, but it was all poppycock. Even if Julian's heart weren't made of stone, he was a duke, and peers did not marry for love. His future wife would be a perfectly proper highborn lady with land and a dowry and a healthy self-interest in becoming a duchess.

It wasn't love, but it would have to be enough.

CHAPTER 2

Dust motes danced in the bright sunlight streaming through the narrow windows as Unity Thorne stepped back to admire her work.

"Good God, Mabel," Rhoda breathed in awe. "You look hideous."

"Don't respond," Unity warned Mabel. "Your prosthetic chin needs time to set."

The King's Theatre wouldn't open to the public for another hour, but there was much to do before the afternoon performance of *Macbeth*. All of the actresses each had her own beautification toilette, but Unity was in charge of turning them into someone else entirely.

Unity moved Mabel a few feet to the right to make room for her next charge. The grand salon for the audience brimmed with luxury and excess, but the cramped little room where Unity performed her magic with cosmetics was barely large enough to house four stools and a mirror. She needed natural light to do her job well.

She also needed fresh air in order to do her job *comfortably*, but the windows were nailed shut... either to bar thieves from entering, or to deter the theatre's property from walking out.

Not that a few nails stopped the actresses from borrowing an unneeded gown or a fine pair of gloves from time to time.

"Gladys, you're next." Unity arranged the second stool where the light was best and motioned for the actress to take her seat.

Gladys cast a dubious look at Mabel. "I don't know about these prosthetics. Mabel *does* look hideous."

"You're the three witches of Macbeth," Unity reminded her.

"But we weren't this hideous yesterday," Gladys insisted. "You can't even tell who we are beneath the noses and the chins and the black wigs."

"Oh, *sit*," Rhoda said in exasperation. "We'll look like witches today and be more memorable than ever." She lowered her voice, despite only the four of them fitting in the small room. "Gladys is between protectors at the moment. She's worried about what the gentlemen might think."

Ah. A valid concern.

"The gentlemen don't make their offers during the show," Unity reminded Gladys. "I will personally redo your cosmetics after the last bow, faster than the audience can vacate their seats. By the time wealthy would-be lovers reach backstage, you'll be the most beautiful actress in the theatre."

"Oy!" Mabel smacked Unity's hip. "Mrrph blerfle!"

"Don't talk," Unity reminded her. "Five more minutes until the glue sets."

"How *do* you think of such clever things?" Rhoda said with admiration.

Unity shrugged. She couldn't help but think of things. Her brain never stopped churning out new ideas.

Gladys shook her head indulgently and took her place on the stool. "You're out of control, Unity."

"Who wants to be controlled?" she replied pertly. "No, thank you. I politely decline."

"You should have declined this position, too," Gladys said. "You barely earn more than the maids who clean the chamber pots."

"Which is an equally important post," Unity pointed out. "How many rich nobs would find themselves in an amorous mood if the theatre smelt of—"

"Mrrgle fergle!" said Mabel.

"She's right." Rhoda leaned over Unity's shoulder to watch her attach the first pros-thetics to Gladys's face. "You're far cleverer than you are paid to be. Every day, I expect to hear that you've found a better position and we shall

all be forced to work with some chit who wouldn't know kohl from a cockerel."

Unity reached for her glue instead of answering. If only acquiring a well-paid position was as simple as having the talent for it!

She would rather *own* a theatre than be in charge of face powder in one. Unity dreamed of having her own building, her own business, her own life to direct as she saw fit. She wished she didn't *need* the two guineas a month from the theatre. It was barely enough coins to clink together.

Worst of all, she *shouldn't* need the theatre! Unity had twice turned someone else's unprofitable disaster into an outrageous success, and all she had to show for it were the scars of betrayal.

Her fingers shook and she forced herself to take a calming breath. She *would* claw her way to financial independence. Someday. Somehow.

And she wouldn't trust anyone but herself to get her there.

"I wish you could be an actress," Rhoda said with a sigh. "We don't get paid much more than you, but it's something."

"I'm a dreadful actress," Unity said, though they all knew her lack of acting skills wasn't the main impediment. Talentless beauties with a powerful enough "sponsor" were given fabulous roles every day.

People like Unity were rarely invited onstage. Not for the big parts. The theatre managers would rather paint up a white actor than give one with brown skin a starring role under the lights.

Women of mixed race, like Unity, often received preferential treatment for their lighter skin. But the most compassionate act the theatre had ever performed for her was to "allow" Unity to apprentice the previous cosmetics artist for a year and a half without pay, until she became skilled enough to replace a higher-earning employee for half of the salary.

Not that top billing was the primary benefit of playing a starring role. The more popular the actress, the wealthier her private patron, but any woman with brains between her ears could find a man willing to pay for her company. For many women, it was the *only* way to keep a roof over their heads and food in their bellies.

Unity liked being some stranger's momentary possession even less than living in her minuscule private room with its squeaky cot and wobbly wooden chair. It was *hers*. And it was temporary.

She *would* find a way out.

"All right, Mabel. You can talk."

"Thank God," Rhoda said. "I am dying to hear all about the masquerade last night."

Unity held a false nose to Gladys's face. "*Mabel* attended the Duke of Lambley's masquerade ball?"

She would have saved Mabel's prosthetics until last, if she'd known. Lambley's hedonistic fêtes were legendary. Unity longed to see what went on inside.

"Not me," Mabel said. "Helene."

Ah. Mabel's sister Helene was Lady Macbeth, the lead actress. She'd paid for Mabel's rented rooms for an entire year with the sale of a single trinket her protector had purchased for her. There had even been money left over for new boots and a fine coat.

All of the other actresses—and, yes, Unity as well—dreamed of asking Helene for an introduction, an invitation, anything. Even one minute inside that glittering world. But such invitations were either too dear to acquire for friends, or Helene simply didn't wish to share the stage... even with her own sister.

"She said it was unspeakably decadent." Mabel eyed her new face in a looking-glass. "It was only her second time to attend, but the footmen remembered her favorite refreshments from the first time and were always on hand with silver trays at the exact moment she craved fresh champagne or fine chocolate."

"But if everyone is masked the entire time, how did they know who she was?" Rhoda asked.

Mabel shrugged. "It's part of the magic. Lambley himself isn't masked. They say he can see right through the masks of others. Perhaps his servants have the same power."

It sounded fanciful to Unity. "Is he really as attractive as they say?"

"Helene says more so." Mabel gave a fluttery sigh. "Not that we'll ever meet him."

That was true enough. Most unmarried gentlemen of the ton took mistresses, but the duke scarcely needed to bother. The most beautiful women in London presented themselves to him every Saturday. There was no need to go shopping when the samples brought themselves to one's door.

"They say his hazel eyes emanate unimaginable heat," said Rhoda.

"They also say he can be unspeakably cold," Unity reminded her.

"Lambley could bark like a dog and still be lusted after," Mabel said. "But he's a sworn bachelor. As untrappable by the ton as he is by the likes of us."

Rhoda shook her head. "He might be sowing his wild oats now, but he's a duke, and by all accounts a good one. He may not be in a hurry, but he'll marry some fancy debutante one day."

Mabel snorted. "She'll never guess about the parties. Ton misses are impossibly sheltered. They wouldn't know what to do with a cock if it sprang up in front of them."

Gladys affected a wholesome voice and widened her eyes. "'Oh dear, whatever could that be? We must summon a surgeon at once, Your Grace! It's swelling at an alarming rate!'"

Laughter filled the tiny room.

"Don't move," Unity scolded Gladys, still grinning. "I'm almost done with your chin. Besides, it's not true and you know it. The reason Lambley's parties are so scandalous is because ladies of the ton *do* attend."

"Maybe that's the kind of woman he wants," Mabel said with a sigh. "A lady on the outside and a harlot on the inside."

"That's what they all want." Gladys's blue eyes twinkled merrily. "We might not personify both roles, but we can offer the best half of the bargain."

"In fact," Mabel said, "after yesterday's show, I met a man who…"

Unity stopped listening to her friends in order to concentrate on applying their cosmetics. Hers wasn't a glamorous post, but it was all that she had and she needed to keep it. For now.

She'd helped others become rich. If she was half as clever as others claimed, she could find a way to do the same for herself.

Oh, not diamonds-and-fur wealthy. Where would she wear such fripperies, anyway? Unity aspired to be just rich enough that she need not worry about money ever again.

The next business she built would be hers to keep. Every brick. Every penny.

Hers, and hers alone.

CHAPTER 3

*U*nity strolled along the pavement down a busy cobblestone street in a so-called undesirable section of London and dreamed of opening her own enterprise right here in her neighborhood.

She didn't mind hard work. It wouldn't even *feel* like work, if it were hers. Oh, there would be tough times and bad days, like with anything else, but no matter what challenges befell her business, it would still be *hers*.

Unfortunately, one couldn't wish such a thing into existence. Businesses required capital. If you didn't have any funds of your own—and, let's face it, she could save her meager theatre wages for the next two centuries and still not accumulate anything resembling "funds"—then what you needed were investors.

Such creatures were almost as impossible to obtain as funds.

Almost.

Unity personally knew two gentlemen with wildly successful businesses. Their businesses were wildly successful because Unity had made them that way. One might think this proven ability would give her cachet and leverage. One would be extremely naïve.

Unity could sneeze out the holy grail itself and she would still be an unmarried, twenty-four-year-old woman with light-brown skin and life savings totaling one hundred and thirty-five guineas, hidden beneath a loose floorboard in a rented apartment. But once upon a time...

The first fool she'd turned into a rich man was her cousin Roger.

Despite being paternal first cousins, Roger had treated his young ward like a maid-of-all-work. As she grew into adolescence, even he could see she possessed something special. Eventually, he'd let her take over the management of his gentlemen's club—as a favor to her, mind you. Don't come asking for extra coins.

Just do what she could to outpace the unfair success of that upstart gaming den in unfashionable Cheapside her cousin despised so much. A lower class establishment with higher popularity simply could not be borne.

Soon, Roger's pitiful club was profitable, and all because of Unity. She reached her majority—and a decision. She would ask her cousin not just for fair wages, but for a commission. After all, the club wouldn't be turning any profit if it weren't for Unity.

Roger answered by kicking her out of his club and out of his home. She had her freedom. She wasn't his ward anymore. If she thought she was such an important kingmaker, well, off she went then to make her own fortune. Roger didn't need a slip of a girl under his expensive heels.

With no money and no references in the middle of winter, some might think her cousin had left Unity with no choice but to take shelter in a brothel, just to have a roof over her head.

But there were sometimes choices, if one knew where to look.

She pulled open the front door of Eshu's Altar and stepped into the smoky, noisy gambling den.

Shouts of "Miss Unity!" rang from all corners, followed immediately by good-natured groans, begging her not to join this table or that, lest she swindle them out of the pot they were surely going to win.

She ignored the whist and faro tables for now, and made her way to the bar instead.

Sampson had a glass of her favorite brandy ready before she reached him. His black hair was cropped short and the deep brown of his jaw freshly shaved. He looked as though he might be off to church—not off to reap a small fortune from the luckless gamblers wagering at the gaming tables.

"Looking lovely today, Miss Unity," Sampson murmured politely.

Unity arched a brow.

"Some men find your general air of fire and brimstone to be lovely," he protested. "It may not be for everyone, but that's why God invented individual taste. What are you furiously thinking about today?"

"My cousin Roger," she admitted.

Sampson grinned and poured himself a matching glass of brandy. "Please tell me he still wakes up every morning despising me."

"He does," Unity promised.

Sampson clinked his glass against hers. "To making our betters jealous."

When Unity had darkened his doorstep for the first time, Sampson Oakes hadn't had the least inkling who her fashionable, self-important cousin was. But he *had* been passingly familiar with Unity's mother, who had grown up not far from Sampson's relatives.

Mother's family had money. Unity's maternal grandfather had built a large church in the neighborhood, and provided affordable loans to enterprising residents who were turned away by the big banks that serviced the ton and the landed gentry.

Mother had said the family money was enough to last for generations. That Unity would live well, and so would her children.

But Grandfather must have given every penny out as loans. Roger said there was no information on how to collect it in the will—or any mention of Unity. He took in his grieving cousin due to familial responsibility but not by choice. He said more than once he wished there was some other cousin she could leech upon. A Black cousin, preferably, to keep her far from Roger's exalted circles.

Unity wished the same thing. She'd felt far more at home in her old neighborhood than she ever did at her cousin's stale residence. If only her church aunts had been related by blood, her life would have turned out differently. Perhaps she would have met Sampson sooner—and not as a homeless beggar.

By some counts, there were ten thousand free Blacks in London, and by other counts twenty thousand. A big number, scattered throughout a big city, and yet oftentimes, it still managed to feel like a small community, where everyone knew everyone else—or knew someone who did.

Sampson hadn't been looking to hire a new maid. Unity hadn't wanted to *be* a maid. She wanted to help him attract more clients than his gambling den could handle. Sampson didn't have a man of business. Unity didn't have a home. In exchange for room and board, she'd prove her worth, if he'd just give her a month's grace to try.

He gave her three months. Then six. Then a year. By then, his gaming establishment was the most frequented in Cheapside and he didn't need Unity's help anymore.

She'd hoped he'd offer her a job.

Instead, he'd offered her marriage.

Sampson was kind and clever and handsome, but Unity was not in the market for a man. If a woman married, the husband would own *her*. No matter how much Unity helped in the gaming hell, it would never be hers. She would always be the assistant, not the one in charge.

So she'd left. Despite there being no contract requiring him to do so, Sampson had settled a tidy sum on her nonetheless, in appreciation of her work.

What coin was left was hidden beneath a floorboard. Unity sipped her brandy. She needed to stop thinking and start *doing* before all she had left to show for her dreams was a blank space in the dust under her rented floor.

"Thank you." Brandy in hand, she strolled through the gaming hell just like she used to do. Besides her, the only other women were serving maids.

"It's Miss Unity!"

"Don't let her sit with us. She'll take our money... *again*."

"I fold, I fold!"

Despite their teasing protests, gentlemen made room for her at each table she passed. Her face was as familiar as the Queen of Diamonds'. More importantly, Sampson had declared Miss

Unity to have a lifetime seat at the table of her choice, and she had taken him up on this promise on several memorable occasions.

Sometimes the hole beneath her floor held far more than one hundred and thirty-five guineas.

But gambling was for pigeons. No matter how talented you were, luck ruled the table at the end. Unity preferred to rely on skill.

One of the gamblers gave her a gap-toothed smile. "What's a hoyden like you doing in a hell like this?"

She rolled her eyes and kept walking. She wasn't a hoyden or a spinster or any other such label. Those were names given to people who had expectations. The only person who expected anything from Unity was herself.

And she was the only person she could rely on to achieve it.

She would make her own way and become financially independent at any cost, come what may. Unity had sworn to never again rely on any man for anything but company. There was nothing she cherished more than her freedom.

"Well?" Sampson appeared at her side, a towel folded over one arm. "Are we falling apart without you?"

"You're doing fine," she assured him.

Eshu's Altar was flourishing. Unlike her cousin Roger, Sampson had paid close attention to everything Unity did or suggested. They had learned from each other.

Cousin Roger's club, the Wit & Whistle, on the other hand... Well. Within a year after Unity's departure, its popularity was already waning. Last she heard, he'd gone through three men of business last season alone and was barely staying afloat.

Unity *might* have whispered a few choice tidbits into gossips' ears to help the process along.

She would not be sorry.

"What do you know about the Duke of Lambley?" she asked Sampson.

His coffee-brown eyes widened. "This isn't his haunt."

She wrinkled her nose. "White's? Boodle's?"

"The Cloven Hoof."

Now that was interesting. The Cloven Hoof was a larger, more infamous gambling den. It was located on the literal edge of the fashionable district, and its clientele spanned the divide between the classes. No truly fashionable lords frequented the establishment, but she was unsurprised to hear someone as unconventional as Lambley would rub elbows with the lower classes. From all accounts, his parties were just as eclectic.

"What do you know about his masquerades?" she asked.

"Is that your next venture?" Sampson's brows lifted. "You're going to compete with the Duke of Lambley?"

"It's not competing if we cater to separate

audiences," she replied. "I'll be competing against you."

Sampson grinned. "I'm not certain this is a masquerade crowd."

"And I am certain there are men and women in Cheapside who would love to attend such an event," Unity answered. "When Vauxhall hosts a masquerade, one can hardly wade through all the people in attendance. Many of whom are thieves and footpads. A masquerade *club* for the common folk could offer a secure environment at a comfortable price."

"It does sound like it would do well," Sampson admitted. "Knowing you, you've already fathomed out every aspect."

She shook her head. "I'm still gathering information. I know what Vauxhall's parties are like firsthand, but I've never attended a private masquerade."

"Well... there are private masquerades, and then there are *private masquerades*." Sampson gave her a sidelong glance. "I'm sure you've heard rumors of the goings-on at the duke's residence?"

Her cheeks heated. "I wouldn't copy *that* part."

"Yes, you would," Sampson said. "If it was the most profitable, most efficient, or most likely to be what the people want. You'll do whatever makes you the most successful. You can't help it. You give your all."

Yes. Well. This time, she'd be giving her all

for *herself* for a change. Creating her own legacy. Controlling her own future.

"How would you like to be the first investor in a new business opportunity?" she asked.

Sampson made a face. "We're widening Eshu's Altar. I won't have a spare penny for at least six months. By then, your public masquerade hall will be the only reason anyone comes to London."

Damn it. Unity forced a smile. She wished his words were true. It *could* have come true. But Sampson was the only wealthy person she knew—and trusted. She wanted to partner with someone from this neighborhood.

Unity had stumbled in here all those years ago out of necessity and out of revenge. Cousin Roger had turned her out into the street without a care. She had wanted to make him pay. This venue was the one he despised above all others. The one he had resented being better than his.

Helping Sampson had been a wonderful start. Helping *herself*... ahh. Her future success as an independent club owner would be the sweetest revenge.

But first, she had to learn everything there was to know about operating a successful masquerade. The sort people would do anything to attend. She knew from experience that the best way to learn was from the thick of things. If she wanted to start a club that rivaled Lambley's balls in popularity... then she needed to become very familiar with Lambley's balls.

"You're making the face," Sampson said. "The *I-will-destroy-all-competition* face."

"You said it wasn't competing," she reminded him. "The duke and I shall be... colleagues."

"Does *he* know that?" Sampson said doubtfully.

Unity handed him her empty glass and straightened her bonnet. "He's about to."

CHAPTER 4

On Monday afternoon, Unity wrangled her voluminous black curls into subdued twists and clothed herself in her finest day dress. She looked more like a governess than a society miss, but she wished to *learn* from the Duke of Lambley, not waltz with him.

How many masquerades would he permit her to attend? If she were lucky... maybe two. It was not at all ideal, but if one was the best she could negotiate, then it would have to do. She'd bring a reticule large enough to hold a journal and several pencils, and take note of absolutely everything.

Her confidence wavered.

She'd spent years observing her cousin's operations before attempting to meddle, and months immersed in Sampson's before daring to make changes. Did she really think a single night hosted by the Duke of Lambley would have the power to—

Yes. She did think. After all, she knew what a masquerade *was*. She had attended several at Vauxhall and elsewhere. All she was looking for was the special spark that made his so different.

It couldn't just be the carnal assignations rumored to proliferate at his parties. London had plenty of brothels and street prostitutes and high class demimondaines for all tastes and pocketbooks. Nor was Lambley the only member of the beau monde to host a masquerade.

Of course, fine gentlemen weren't *supposed* to host parties. There was meant to be a wife or a dowager or an aunt or a sister acting as hostess, to make the gathering respectable. But clearly the duke wasn't too concerned with conforming to society's expectations.

That was the only reason Unity might have a chance. *She* did not match Polite Society's expectations. To them, she was the wrong color, the wrong class, the wrong everything. But to Lambley, who delighted in being unconventional...

One night. One invitation. It could happen.

When the hack drew up outside the duke's grand residence, Unity froze with her gloved fingers against the smudged glass of the small window.

The house was enormous. Three stories tall, and wide enough to fit her cousin's club and Sampson's gambling parlor in each wing. What on earth did anyone do with that much house?

He could turn the first two floors into a theatre and still have more living space than a normal person would know what to do with.

Perhaps that's what he *was* doing. Masquerades were a sort of theatre. Costumes to wear, roles to play. She could not wait to see what the stage looked like up close.

Unity handed the driver a coin and scrambled out of the hackney, then immediately regretted having done so. A lady did not *scramble*. Not that she was likely to be confused for a lady, but nonetheless, she did not wish to create a poor impression. What if he had seen her ungainly leap to the cobbled street?

More importantly, how was this street so *clean*? Did he and his neighbors employ an army of sweepers to dust away every pebble and leaf and horse dropping before it could even land? Did shoe-shiners pop out of the shadows to buff individual cobblestones into gleaming perfection after each carriage passed?

She made her way up the gorgeous, trimmed path to the front door, pausing every few feet to gawk at the size and breadth of his home.

Only because she was staring slack-jawed and shameless did she see a figure step close enough to one of the enormous windows for his face to be bathed in sunlight.

Three seconds. Maybe four. But that was all it took to burn that patrician profile into Unity's brain for the rest of time. He was not even the sort of man she *liked*, and she would no doubt dream of him every night for the next two months.

Tall and wide of shoulder, dressed in the first stare of fashion and all that other twaddle Unity didn't care about. It should have made him indistinguishable from every other rich, indolent Town buck.

But that face. Those shameless wenches had told her he was attractive, but a mere word could not encapsulate the harsh beauty of his face.

The duke's visage should not have been handsome at all. Pale, cruel, unyielding. The angles a touch too sharp, the jaw a touch too square... and yet, touching was indeed what she longed to do. Feel those harsh lines beneath her fingertips. The firm lips of his unsmiling mouth, the dark lashes framing eyes that...

He had been too far away to gauge their color. His expression had not been angry or pinched or brooding, but rather... calculating, perhaps. As though when he looked out of his window, he did not see luxurious homes on a fairy-tale-perfect street, but rather the next battle in a war. He was moving chess pieces in his mind, and London's lords and ladies were his pawns.

Definitely not an attractive look, she assured herself. He exuded coldness and power and control. A god, dispassionately surveying his creations, and deciding what to toy with next.

By the flutter in Unity's pulse and the shallowness in her wispy breaths, she had no doubt every woman who crossed his threshold hoped to be the next morsel on the menu.

Indeed, this was the quickest reconnaissance mission she had ever attempted. She hadn't even made it all the way to the front door, and already she knew exactly why the female half of his guests would strike any bargain required to be allowed through the door. Hell, even some of the male guests likely felt the same way.

The duke's magnetism was the sort where you knew—you *knew*—he was bad for you in every sense, but it only made you want to press even closer. To be the one that haughty face turned towards, to be the butterfly pinned by those all-knowing eyes.

She swallowed and hastened up the path before she lost her nerve.

A butler opened the door.

Did she curtsey? She curtseyed. Why did she curtsey? Roger had a butler, and she never curtseyed for *him*. Then again, she'd felt as though they were of the same class. Servants and wards weren't humans in the eyes of Roger.

This butler, however. He didn't seem like an employee at all. He seemed regal. A marble statue, like his master. Cold. Dispassionate. Waiting.

"Er," Unity said. "I... came to see... the duke?"

"Have you an appointment?" the butler asked in a tone that implied they both knew she did not have an appointment.

Unity fought the urge to fidget, then went ahead and fidgeted. This was her *best* dress, her *best* bonnet. Was it the light brown of her skin? Or was "respectable governess" the mistake? Perhaps the duke had a personal policy never to meet with anyone who could be considered proper.

Or perhaps it was her extended gaping in the front garden that had given her away.

"I've no appointment." She straightened her pelisse. "I'm here to beg just a moment of His Grace's time. My name is—"

The butler held out his hand.

Unity stared at it. Was she supposed to shake it? Kiss it? Dance a reel?

The butler's voice was impassive. "Your calling card, if you please."

Her *calling* card. Of course. She would absolutely hand one over, if she'd ever had reason to own such a thing prior to this moment.

"If you could just... *tell* him..." She trailed off. It was clear that one did not "tell" His Grace anything. If she were meant to be here, she would have an appointment, and they both knew it.

The butler lowered his hand. "If there's nothing else?"

"Nothing else," Unity mumbled and turned away before he could close the door in her face.

Lambley had won this round, damn him. But the game had just started.

THE FOLLOWING MORNING, Unity had the hackney driver drop her off two streets away. Today, she would not be strolling down the immaculate pavement like a country bumpkin on her first visit to the city. The front door was not the way in.

She was heading for the back.

Unity no longer looked out of place in the duke's fancy neighborhood. With her black dress and her starched apron and the mobcap hiding her hair from view, she looked exactly like any number of servants staffing the huge households. On this street, people like her outnumbered people like him twenty-to-one.

Her mistake had been trying to approach him as an equal. She was not his equal. Not only wasn't she a lady, she also wasn't a member of the land-owning class, or the dreaded nouveau riche whose fortunes were made in the mills and manufactories.

Unity wasn't only good at coaxing businesses to higher efficiency and value. She was damn good with a broom and a mop as well. Once she was hired on as a maid, she would be able to inspect every corner of the ballroom as closely as she liked without anyone blinking an eye.

Better yet, she would be *invisible*. She could stand an arm's length from any given lord or lady without her presence registering in their minds at all. There could not be a better vantage point from which to conduct her research.

Then she would go back to Cheapside and open her masquerade club for the common folk once Sampson was in a position to be a founding investor. What had he said—six months? That was more than enough time to have every aspect of the Duke of Lambley's weekly masquerades memorized.

Unity grinned to herself. She was close now. Her assembly rooms wouldn't just be the joy of Cheapside. They'd be her future. The permanence she'd sought all her life. The income with which to secure it. The respect she'd longed for.

And it would be *hers*.

The moment her club was profitable enough to repay her debt to Sampson, she would do so. After that, no more partners. She wouldn't need one. Unity was perfectly capable on her own. Yes, yes, all of her friends pestered her about when she planned to get married.

After she'd proven herself and secured her own future, she'd consider the idea. But not until that day... and perhaps never at all.

Once she was financially secure and fully independent, why bother ruining a good thing by taking a husband? If she wanted to share her bed from time to time, well, there were less permanent ways to find pleasure than giving up her freedom for a man.

She smoothed her spotless apron and knocked briskly at the servant's entrance.

At once, a wigged footman opened the door. Unity frowned. She had been expecting a maid. Had this tall young man in blue-and-gold livery been stationed at the servants' entrance like a butler? Or had he just been passing by?

She gave him her brightest smile. "May I speak to the housekeeper please? I'm here to enquire about a post."

"There are no open posts," the footman answered.

Unity blinked. No open posts? In a house of this size? There was always room for a maid to take over for this or that person who was ill or incompetent.

She kept her smile in place. "If I could just speak to Mrs..."

The footman arched a brow. "Do you have a card?"

Did she have a—no, she did not have a card! She wagered this sanctimonious footman didn't have a bloody card either. What sort of maid wandered about printing calling cards that cost more than her monthly wages?

She hesitated. *Did* rich people have rich servants? *Might* Jane in the scullery have a crisp stack of embossed cards reading, "Jane, Scullery"? Was Unity completely out of her depth?

"I am sorry to have wasted your time," she said tightly and turned away with a bit more flounce than was truly necessary.

Was this a house or a military compound? Surely there was *some* way to get inside.

Second round: Lambley.

But these were still opening moves. He had not won yet. She was still learning her opponent. Every man had his weakness.

All she had to do was find it.

It took three days—and the aid of Rhoda, Mabel, and Gladys—to put together the pieces of her plan.

On Friday afternoon, she stepped out of a hackney and onto the duke's pristine cobblestone street adorned in a stunning, low-cut crimson gown that would not have looked out of place in an Italian opera.

Possibly because it was part of the lead soprano's wardrobe.

The sweeping, clinging satin and silk were also the sort of materials one might expect to find draped seductively about one of the many voluptuous demimondaines who plied their trade off stage and during intermissions.

She was through with proper comportment and attempts at honest labor. Her friends claimed all men were the same, and that the quickest way to their heart was by displaying one's cleavage.

Unity didn't want the duke's cold, frivolous heart. She wanted one evening on the other side of this bloody door for a single, solitary masquerade.

This had to work.

The white-haired butler opened the front door and stared. Not at Unity's face—which she'd altered slightly with cosmetics—but at her bosom, which was more outside of her bodice than in.

"M-may I..." he stammered.

She beamed at him, not that he was watching. "I'm here to see His Grace."

He swallowed. "I... Do you..."

She opened a bejeweled reticule and dramatically produced the single gilded calling card she'd had printed just that morning, which read:

Miss Unity Thorne
Courtesan

THE BUTLER'S wide blue eyes nearly rolled out of his pale head.

Did courtesans carry calling cards? And if so, did they state their nocturnal profession? Who knew? Who cared? Despite the wildness of the duke's weekly parties, Lambley was infamous for never bedding the same woman twice, and being agnostic to race or class. He had never bedded Unity—nor would he. But he was bound to want to try.

Heroically, the butler managed to drag his gaze from Unity's over-plumped bosom up to her eyes. "Do you have an appointment with His Grace?"

"Trust me." She winked. "He wants one."

"One moment, please." Clutching her card, the older man barely remembered to shut the door before dashing off to find his master.

If the butler recognized Unity—which was doubtful—he'd think her proper governess attire had been the costume. No respectable lady would show up dressed like this. Even the courtesans limited such flamboyant frippery to the dim light of starlit evenings and flickering chandeliers.

She'd considered using a false name, but the duke seemed the sort who might exhaustively investigate his guests prior to granting an invitation. He would not find a list of prior clients, but he *would* discover a woman who had simultaneously once been young and homeless. It would not take much imagination to presume she'd risen from poverty by selling her body, as so many had done.

Especially not with a calling card like that in his hand.

She was not one of the famous courtesans written about breathlessly in the society columns. The ones fought over by earls, dueled over by viscounts. The ones whose accessories and hair arrangements were copied by the same fine ladies who pretended not to know their aristocratic husbands spent their nights in the arms of a paid mistress.

The Duke of Lambley had no wife to lie to about his whereabouts to, and was well known for befriending fashionable demimondaines and inviting them to his masquerades. According to rumor, the more popular the courtesan, the more likely she might be chosen as one of Lambley's infamous single-night affairs.

Unity had no intention of becoming a conquest, but she was not above offering her bosom as bait if it allowed her across the threshold. He would be more open to a working woman than to a highborn title-hunting debutante.

Presenting herself as a courtesan made Unity ineligible to be his duchess, which would also ease his mind about allowing her in. At worst, she was after a spot of fun and a bit of gold, not a trip to the altar. Exactly the sort of woman who would enjoy a hedonistic masquerade.

And she would indeed enjoy it! Every minute would bring her closer to her goals of financial security and full independence. That was, provided the duke cared to—

The door swung open wide and the butler gestured expansively. "If you'll follow me, madam."

Unity's legs trembled. It was not yet checkmate, but this round had gone to her. She hoped.

Into the lair she went.

CHAPTER 5

Julian had been about to bite into his second tea cake when Barnaby entered the parlor in a flush.

"You have a visitor," his butler announced.

Julian arched a brow.

"I know that you're busy," Barnaby said quickly. "But I did not want to send the young... er... person... away without consulting you. She... she..." The butler flushed and placed a calling card on the dining table next to Julian's tea cup.

She, indeed.

Julian hadn't thought it possible for his already raised brows to climb even higher, but here he was, staring at an extremely unlikely calling card.

"What does she want?"

"A meeting with you."

"Obviously. But what does she *want?*"

"Er..." The butler coughed into his gloved

hand. "She implied the answer to that question is whatever *you* want, Your Grace."

An intriguingly indecent offer that Barnaby apparently believed the duke ought to consider taking.

Julian had never and would never employ a mistress, a stance which some courtesans seemed to take as a personal challenge. However, those women tended to already know him and his proclivities. He had never heard of a Unity Thorne.

Something else had brought her here. Money, most likely.

The promise of luxury was what brought everyone to his door. He could listen to her entreaty, and perhaps give her a banknote or two before sending her on her way.

Or, if she struck him as the right sort, perhaps he'd invite her to tomorrow's masquerade instead and allow her to fish in an even deeper pond.

"Show her into the green salon." Julian glanced at the tall-case clock. "I will be there in seven and a half minutes."

Despite his unquenched curiosity, no one controlled the duke's time but the duke. Tea ended precisely at four o'clock. Miss Thorne had already disrupted Julian's repast enough.

"I shall see to it, Your Grace." Barnaby bowed and closed the door behind him as he left.

Julian returned his attention to his cakes and

his newspaper, putting the unusual interruption from his mind. The dining room was perfectly silent. The footmen in the shadows did not speak. His servants were paid to attend their posts, a task they did very well, and for which labor they were rewarded handsomely.

All non-masquerade days were exactly the same. He awoke at a precise hour, bathed and dressed at a precise hour, broke his fast at a precise hour, attended to his correspondence at a precise hour, took his tea at a precise hour, met with his man of business at a precise hour, and so on.

Everything in Julian's life unfolded just as he planned it. Even the gossip about him was divine. Last week's masquerade had been phenomenal. People were still whispering allusions to entertainments that could not be spoken aloud.

The notoriety greatly reduced the amount of correspondence the duke must deal with. He received plenty of invitations, although not to any of the truly proper things. Which was too bad, he supposed. He might have liked Almack's. There were rules there.

The invitations Julian received were to the sorts of unorthodox affairs where anything might happen. He tossed them all into a large basin for his man of business to politely decline, as he had for years.

Julian didn't want "anything" to happen. He wanted the things he carefully orchestrated and *only* the things he carefully orchestrated to occur.

Such as the business of finding a wife.

This was the last year for masquerades. Julian turned thirty-five next year, and he had long planned to have a wife by that age, and beget his heir by the following spring. It was all there in his journal.

He took his position in the House of Lords seriously and expected his son to do the same. This meant raising his children as part of society, which meant Julian had a reputation to mend... right after this season. He would make these last masquerades the most memorable of all, and then settle down to the business of selecting a proper, impeccable, predictable wife.

All he had to do was orchestrate the perfect marriage and the perfect heirs and the perfect family just like he structured every other aspect of his life. He could do it.

Not every lady wished for a husband whose name graced the scandal columns as often as Julian's, but the vast majority of young ladies would overlook quite a bit if it meant nabbing a wealthy duke. All that nonsense about reformed rakes making the best husbands.

Julian had no intention of being a romantic husband. Romance was unpredictable, and he had neither the time nor the patience for such folderol. All he required was a union of convenience.

What was marriage if not a masquerade? He

could design and manage it as well as any other. He'd select a biddable wife, who would bear well-behaved sons, who would take their rightful place in society without disrupting the duke's life one whit.

This unexciting future was what he would have, because it was all he *could* have. He was not capable of love, so there was no sense pretending to seek it.

Julian set down his napkin and rose to his feet. It was time to make sense of the courtesan in his sedate green parlor.

He left the calling card on the table and strode down the corridor and into the drawing room, intending to inform Miss Thorne that—

Well, he wasn't certain what he might have informed her. He had *planned* a stern speech. He planned everything. But when he saw her, all of the carefully chosen words evaporated from his head.

She was tall for a woman. Voluptuous. The scarlet opera gown she wore at four o'clock in the afternoon simultaneously hugged every curve whilst also managing to swirl lushly over his understated Axminster carpet.

Her skin was a light golden brown, darker than tea with milk but not quite dark enough as to be chestnut. A great deal of soft skin was on display. Her neck was bare, her arms were bare, and her bodice—well. He could certainly see what had scrambled Barnaby's brain. Julian's throat had also gone uncomfortably dry.

Miss Thorne's full lips were painted as red as her gown, an affectation that was not remotely fashionable, and yet constricted his tight chest further. A beauty spot beckoned just to the left of her mouth. Her nose was wide and pert, her cheekbones high and flushed, and her eyes... were drinking him in with much the same expression he imagined displayed on his own face.

Her black lashes were long, her eyelids sleepy, but her clear brown eyes were quick and alert. A profusion of black ringlets spilled over her forehead and down her neck from an upswept coiffure dripping with pearls.

No—not *real* pearls. Julian could tell the difference from here. Perhaps in the dim light of evening, one would be fooled, but here in his parlor, beneath three enormous windows brimming with bright sunshine, Miss Thorne looked...

Disreputable and utterly ravishing.

"Miss Thorne," he said.

He expected her to curtsey. Perhaps to coo or to flutter or whatever she thought would best sell the wares she had on display.

Instead, she attacked him.

Not physically. She did not move from her position in the center of his parlor. She didn't have to. She unleashed a whirlwind of words, pelting him at all angles until he squinted against their force like a wanderer lost in a sandstorm.

"Here we are, Your Grace, and I am certain

you're wondering why that would be. Or perhaps you're not, because you think you know why I'm here, and are eager to get to the business of it, in which case I must swiftly inform you that your access to my body shall be limited to your handsome eyes because I have come for another reason entirely. Your masquerades."

"My what?" he said, his tone sharp with warning.

She smiled, not cowed by him in the least, which was unprecedented and infuriating. His ability to command a room just by being in it was a trick he had cultivated into a fine art and had never before failed him.

"Your masquerades," she repeated.

He ignored this. "Back to the subject of business," he said in his coldest voice, looking down the bridge of his nose at her from his greater height. "I am not in the market for a mistress."

"And I am not in the market for a master," she replied in a tone that said, *There, now that we've had done with your little topic, shall we get on with mine?*

He did not like it at all.

"You presume to barge into my home and demand an invitation to the most exclusive ton event from no less than the Duke of Lambley himself?"

"It's not a 'ton' event if the majority of guests could not be greeted without their masks," she replied, "and I find your unsubtle switch to third person adorably pretentious. I'm quite aware you're the sixth Duke of Lambley and that you outrank all but royalty and your two dozen fellow dukes. Congratulations. You did nothing to achieve it. You did, however, make this town infinitely more interesting the moment you threw your first masked ball."

A muscle worked at his temple. He was mortally offended and disproportionately flattered, all at the same time.

"I'm here to help you," she said.

"Help... *me?*" he managed.

"Your masquerades are wonderful, I'm told. Although, yes, I'd need an invitation in order to develop my own opinion firsthand. 'Wonderful' is... *acceptable*, perhaps, to some, but you don't seem the sort of man who prides himself on 'acceptable', and *I* am the sort of woman who can improve anything, if given the chance to try."

"You want an invitation to one of my parties so that you can... give your unsolicited opinion about them?"

"I am recommending you solicit said opinion posthaste, but more importantly, my opinion is only the beginning. I will find every last imperfection and offer a comprehensive solution to improve it. Much like cleaning a copper pot with lemon and a bit of salt, your masquerades will shine so bright, they'll hurt the eyes."

"You want to *change* them?" he sputtered in disbelief.

This woman didn't just want to elbow her way in where she wasn't invited, she planned to inject a measure of unpredictability into a thing he'd fashioned into being exactly what he wanted.

"No," he said firmly. "Unthinkable. Impossible."

"There, there," she said in a tone so patronizing he could practically *feel* her slender fingers patting the top of his head. "I am certain dukes are never told of their faults, no matter how many there must be, but I am not here to critique *you*. By all accounts, your masquerades are the best in England, which is not a thing that happens by accident. You want them to be superlative. I want to help you make them even better than that. You don't seem the sort of man to brook any sort of shortcoming. If I were to discern one... wouldn't you wish to address it?"

Of course he would.

He glared at her. She was not impressed by his title, but she *was* impressed by his parties—and thought they could become even more impressive. With her help.

He didn't want or need her help!

But... he *did* want this final season of masquerades to be the most memorable he had ever thrown.

Miss Thorne's expression was earnest. "All you need... is a lady's touch."

He snorted. "Are you a lady?"

"A woman's touch," she amended, unperturbed by the dig.

It wasn't a dig, he realized. It was truth. Only someone of his class would be offended at being considered lower than a lord or lady. Miss Thorne was nothing at all like—

Nothing like him.

Intriguing.

He had not sought an outside opinion, but he could not find one further afield from peers and peeresses than the red-lipped woman standing in the middle of his parlor.

"What if I told you this was my last year for masquerades?" he said. "Perhaps I am no longer interested in such indecorous amusements because I am on the hunt for a wife."

She shrugged. "What if I told you that you might find your future wife under this very roof, smitten thanks to the improvements we're about to undertake?"

"I would laugh at your naivety," he said, and did just that. "The kind of lady I'm looking for would never attend such saturnalia."

"I laugh at *your* naivety," she said, and made an equal show of doing so. "I thought you said these were ton parties. Perhaps only a handful of guests have bowed before the Queen, but why would you assume that one's comportment whilst anonymous is the same as when promenading with your precious peers? Whatever kind of woman you want your wife to be, she can be that *and* attend a masquerade at the same time."

No. She would not be innocent and pure after attending one of Julian's masquerades. But did he *want* innocent and pure? Or did he want a wife he might have something in common with? A marriage in which both parties could tolerate each other's company?

The option had not occurred to him.

He'd had an intended once. Long ago. He hadn't picked her. Their fathers had declared the match. Julian had been eight years old. Too young to understand about marriage, but old enough to know he didn't want *that* girl with the runny nose and the tendency to knock over all of his belongings.

One day, instead of going on a picnic with the two families, Julian had thrown an unholy fit instead. Father had locked him in his bed-chamber and told Julian he was to be deprived of all future entertainments until he got control of himself.

Sudden rainfall and the unexpected collapse of an old bridge prevented the others from ever coming home. Eight-year-old Julian's wish to make his own decisions was granted at the cost of his family.

He got control of himself.

Eventually.

And then never, ever relinquished that control again.

He would wrest control of this situation, too. He could grant Miss Thorne an invitation. What harm would it do? He could rescind her welcome at any time. If he did not like what she had to say, he did not have to listen. *He* was the one with the power. Just as he liked it.

"Tomorrow night," he said. "Ten o'clock. My night butler will be expecting you."

"Tomorrow and every Saturday," she countered. "I am talented, but not a miracle worker. I will need time to familiarize myself with every detail before I can be expected to—"

"Tomorrow night. Ten o'clock," he enunciated. "Your continued presence will be determined on a minute-by-minute basis. Our agreement ends the day I'm betrothed or the moment you disappoint me, whichever comes first."

She stared at him.

Speechless? Miss Thorne? He was glad to see something could achieve it. "I suppose you expect to be paid for your so-called 'expertise' overseeing a party you've never attended?"

"First night free," she said quickly, having found her voice again. "To prove to you I possess the skills I claim to have. After that, I think a weekly rate of..."

She named a number that was laughably small for him, but he supposed comparable to what an accomplished courtesan might gather in monthly presents from her patrons. Miss

Thorne intended to take advantage of his wealth, but not extort it. Asking just enough for it to be a windfall for her, whilst being negligible to him.

She was clever. He would give her that. And presumptuous, which was a less positive trait. Whether she would prove herself any good to him remained to be seen.

"Not a minute past ten o'clock or your name will be crossed from the list." He turned on his heel. "Barnaby will show you out."

"Barna—who?"

The pink-cheeked butler swept into the room from his position just outside the open doorway. "If you'll come with me, madam?"

"But I still—"

Julian could barely hear them. He was striding too quickly to the room adjacent to his study, where his man of business sat at a large desk.

"Mr. Voss," the duke said briskly. "There's been a change in plans."

"Change?" Voss stared at him. "*You?*"

"It's the same plan," Julian admitted. "Marriage by thirty-five. I've decided to implement my bride hunt concurrently with the most outrageous masquerades of my tenure."

"Concurrently, Your Grace?" his man of business stammered.

Julian nodded at the basin of invitations upon Voss's desk. "As you politely decline, if the recipient is at all connected to the beau monde, feel free to casually divulge that His Grace is finally on the hunt for a bride."

"If I do that," Voss said carefully, "they will all descend upon you like locusts."

"No." Julian smiled. "Only the ones who don't mind a little debauchery."

CHAPTER 6

The next evening, as Julian strode through his wide, empty ballroom, the air felt charged with electricity, like a summer night just before a storm.

Everything was in place, exactly as he liked it. Exactly as he'd *planned* it. The first guests would arrive within the hour. Ten o'clock sharp. Already a queue of carriages was forming. They knew the rules. No one allowed in before ten; no one allowed to remain past dawn.

Which meant, the only way to maximize one's limited time at the masquerade was to be one of the first through the door.

He made his way there now. The night butler installed himself at nine thirty. Julian pulled open the door to the receiving chamber and paused halfway across the threshold.

Fairfax was not alone.

Miss Unity Thorne was chatting with him in the vestibule. She wore a glittering emerald mask with tall, golden feathers, but there was no disguising her beauty. That warm honey voice, that soft caramel skin, that sole beauty mark near those berry-red lips...

"You're early."

He couldn't see her arch a brow, but he could hear it in her voice. "You said not to be late."

Fairfax's mask did not cover his lips, which were smirking in obvious amusement.

"Where is your mask?" Miss Thorne asked Julian.

"I don't wear one."

"He wouldn't want to be mistaken for anything other than king of the castle," Fairfax said helpfully.

Julian glowered at him.

Miss Thorne eyed him appreciatively. "I doubt anyone could mistake our duke for anything other than who and what he is."

Somehow, this managed to sound like both a compliment and a condemnation.

"No more bothering the night butler." Julian turned back toward the empty ballroom. "Follow me."

He did not wait to see if she would. He knew the answer. People always followed him. Tease as she liked, Miss Thorne wanted to be granted entrée more than Julian needed to give it. Per the terms he had laid out, he could terminate this arrangement at any moment.

Indeed, perhaps he ought to. She was not just a distraction to the entirely too-amused-for-his-own-good night butler. Miss Thorne was also a distraction to Julian himself.

Not that his habitual pre-party inspection required deep concentration. They had been doing things the same way for years. By now, his servants could prepare the refreshments and arrange the furniture blindfolded. His balls were scandalous, but dependable.

He paused at the first refreshment table and turned to explain its location and replenishment schedule.

Miss Thorne was not at his side.

She had stopped in her tracks a few feet in from the door and was staring about the ballroom with her mouth hanging open in astonishment. She'd even removed her mask, in order to better goggle at the sparkling crystal chandeliers, the gleaming marble floor, the gold-plated everything.

Julian shifted his weight and tried to see the room through her wondering eyes. He could not. This had always been his home. One of his many homes. He was wealthy even by the standards of the ton, but he was hardly the only peer whose residence was awash in crystal and marble and gold.

He could not recall the last time he had gawked at anything. As for his guests... Julian knew his ballroom was impressive. He cultivated it to be, just as he arranged everything about the party quarters to be luxurious and hedonistic.

His guests came for that experience, but did not want to be reminded of the particulars. They knew the chandeliers sparkled, but they did not need to know they were equipped with all-fresh candles one hour prior to the doors opening, so that the flames would glow all night without needing to be changed or relit.

They knew the desserts and canapés were delicious and never more than a few steps away, but they did not need to know how the proper placement had been determined for each table, the best angles, the most enticing combinations, the ideal moment to refresh each platter, itself assigned a specific chef who specialized in that specific dish or arrangement.

The dais, with its orchestra. Musicians of the highest quality, two per position, so that they could be switched out as needed for respites and other concerns without ever suffering the slightest break in the music.

They were set up now, waiting for Julian's cue, which would come at ten minutes to ten as it always did, thus providing his approaching guests with the promise of a magical night even before they stepped foot on the dance floor.

But he wasn't certain he had ever seen one of them stop and stare in wonder like Miss Thorne was doing now.

He suddenly yearned to know more about her. Courtesan, she'd said, but not available for him. Why? Was she already some other man's mistress? It was easy enough to believe. One could hardly look at her without wanting her.

Julian was no stranger to dalliances. Those were not distractions, but carefully planned encounters. Partners chosen by him, during ball hours only, the last hour before dawn. When the masquerade ended, everyone would leave—guests, temporary lover, and all. While the sun was still rising, the servants put the house in order and life returned to exactly how it had been before the ball began, just like Julian liked it.

Miss Thorne did not seem to be nearly so ordered an individual. She fairly crackled with impulsiveness, her unguarded expressions right there for the gazing upon. It was not his fault that he could not stop staring.

What sort of life did this black-haired beauty lead? Sheltered enough to be in awe of a ballroom, yet worldly enough to possess multiple sweeping, dramatic gowns fit for the opera. This one was rich sapphire and dotted with "diamonds" that were almost certainly paste, none of which detracted from her beauty.

He longed to feel those soft curves for himself. Beneath his palms, against his hard body. He wanted her to look at him the way she looked at tall silver trays piled with aphrodisiacs. With surprise and wonder and delight and pleasure.

None of which he would be sharing with Miss Thorne. To admit his visceral reaction would make himself vulnerable, a state that Julian did not permit in his life.

Miss Thorne caught him looking at her and flushed, her cheeks going dark. It made for a very fetching sight. She tugged a small journal from her reticule and hastened to his side.

"A thousand apologies." She gave a self-conscious laugh. "What were you saying, Your Grace?"

This time, when he launched into his explanation behind the process leading to this or that element, she listened with rapt attention, looking up from her madly scribbled notes only long enough to gaze intently at whatever detail he was pointing out.

It was almost as if she were dazzled by *him*, he realized. Julian *was* this ballroom. He was every surface and every tray and every drop of champagne. Everything she could see or touch or taste was there because of a decision he'd made. These were his thoughts and plans and wishes come to life.

"This is fascinating," she said as she scribbled. "Have you thought about offering heartier fare, like potato stew?"

Serve...*vegetables?* He stared at her, aghast.

"No, I have not thought about that horror, nor shall I. The very idea proves that you—"

"What about chairs?" she asked. "Should there be more of them? Perhaps over here?"

"No," he said coldly. "The reason we have this

precise number of chairs, located in their current position, is—"

To Miss Thorne's credit, she nodded eagerly and took copious notes on everything Julian explained.

To Miss Thorne's demerit, she questioned *everything*. She could not simply accept that a thing was done a certain way because it was the best way for that thing to be done. She had to poke at it from all angles and ask if he hadn't considered any number of options that he either *had* considered and discarded after careful investigation and trial, or that clearly weren't worth considering in the first place.

"And the musicians," she said. "Why have—"

Why was her favorite question. Fortunately, Julian was more than equal to the task. He liked having concrete answers. There was not a *why* she could ask that he couldn't parry with an in-depth, well-reasoned explanation. From colors to arrangements and styles to scarcity, everything had a reason for being exactly where and how it was, or he would not have permitted its presence in his home to begin with.

"Do you have an answer for everything?" she asked.

"Yes," he answered simply.

She arched her brows. "And must you control everything? Down to the ripeness of the strawberries?"

"Why not?"

The ability hadn't come easy. When the rain

had taken out that rotted bridge and killed everyone in the passing carriages, Julian had not been in control of anything at all. Not himself, not his grief, and not his suddenly upended life.

His uncle became guardian and left the ducal affairs in shambles. Whatever he did all day in his study had more to do with the cheap gin on the sideboard than the correspondence left in towering piles upon the floor. Uncle had loved Julian, had loved his dead brother, but had left that legacy in a shambles.

Julian vowed never to rely on those who "loved" him ever again.

Just because someone meant well did not mean it was good to have them in one's life.

After learning the extent of his uncle's mismanagement, Julian never returned to university. He was needed here. His school was the dukedom. He learned everything there was to know about every property, every tenant, every blade of grass. And he made it all blossom. There was always a right way, which Julian made his mission to find and implement at any cost.

His estate was wealthier than ever. The envy of all. A product of cold calculation and deliberate action.

So, yes. There was a reason for this precise ripeness of strawberries. Any riper, and they risked going soft in the warm air. Any less, and the tartness could overpower the sweetness or undercut the taste altogether.

There was a right way. Julian's way. He left nothing to chance.

That was where he had gone wrong the day he lost his family. He had failed to predict the damage to the bridge in order to prevent disaster. On the other side of the coin, eight-year-old Julian's stubborn insistence on being in charge of himself was what had ended up saving his life.

Control was a safety net against an unpredictable world.

Sometimes, the only dependable means of survival.

"But what about..." Miss Thorne took on a faraway expression, then motioned for a dubious footman to join them. "Could I just see how this trio of chairs would look closer to the dais?"

The footman froze. The lad did not need to look at Julian to know the answer to the question. The footman sent Miss Thorne a wide-eyed, quelling gaze and shook his head urgently before scurrying to retake his position by the champagne fountain.

Miss Thorne stared after him. "What a strange young man."

And with that, she tucked her journal back into her reticule and leaned over to pick up the closest armchair herself.

An army of footmen materialized at her sides, blocking the path and coaxing her arms away from the freshly polished mahogany of the chair.

"What..." Miss Thorne sent a shocked look over her shoulder. "I cannot arrange things to see how they might look?"

"No changes," Julian said sharply.

"How can anyone improve anything without making changes?" she burst out.

"No unnecessary changes," he clarified.

"How will I know if they're unnecessary unless I try them?" she demanded. "I wasn't going to move the chairs permanently unless it *was* an important change. But without seeing the difference—"

"This is the best location for these chairs."

Miss Thorne made a noise in her throat as though debating tossing one of the perfectly placed chairs at his head. "Have you personally tested every possible angle and chair arrangement permutation in this ballroom?"

Julian raised his brows at his footmen.

"Yes, ma'am," they explained earnestly. "Season Two was exhaustively dedicated to seating arrangements."

"Type of chairs, quantity of chairs—"

"Chaises, sofas, stools, divans—"

"Type of material, density of cushions—"

"Arms or no arms—"

"Proper height, proper depth—"

"I see," Miss Thorne said faintly, and left the armchair alone. She pulled out her journal and jotted a note.

Julian doubted she did see.

In the thirteen years his well-meaning uncle had held the purse strings, he'd undone everything Julian's parents and forebears had accomplished. Not out of evilness but incompetency.

Julian had learned the more he cared about someone, the more ability they had to disappoint. And if one wanted a thing done right...well, he had mastered the art of taking the reins himself.

Miss Thorne pursed her lips. "Is there any point in me asking about the wine or the cakes?"

"None."

"What about—"

And off she went, poking at perfection all over again. Julian flexed his fingers in irritation. She wanted to change everything, just like his uncle.

No, that was unfair. Miss Thorne was unlike his uncle. She was trying to work *with* him. To talk to him, to include him, to make it a conversation, cooperation, a partnership.

She listened to him.

And... he supposed he was listening to her. As annoying as her second-guessing of his decisions might be, no one else but him had ever looked about this ballroom and wondered these same things. What *if* the chaises longues, what *if* the pear tarts, what *if* the curtains?

"Are you always this hardheaded?" Miss Thorne groused. "Other people have ideas, too."

This was her first time beneath this roof, and

she was immediately thinking along the same path Julian had taken when he'd turned twenty-two and decided to fill the silence of his cavernous home with occasional masquerades. Wildness that he could control. Perfection he could perform.

"If I seem cold and intractable, it is because I am ruled by my brain, not by my fancy," he replied.

"Humph," she said. "Cold like a burning ember. You're not hard and passionless. The reason you're unwilling to change things is because you *do* care. Far more than the average person, I'd wager."

He glared at her, appalled. Julian had no response to such unsolicited impertinence, so he snapped his fingers toward the orchestra instead. It was nine minutes until ten. Miss Thorne was a bad influence already.

Music filled the air. Elegant music. Classic pieces.

Strings not nearly loud enough to drown out Miss Thorne's continued questions about every aspect of Julian's balls.

Her endless queries outlined many of the same theories and hypotheses Julian had considered as he'd refined his masquerades over the years. While today he had all of the answers, he was forced to admit that if he'd known her back then, she might indeed have saved him quite a bit of time.

But this was now. He didn't want her advice,

and he certainly didn't need her changing things. What he wanted was...

To kiss her. To taste that mouth that never shut up, to silence her tongue by offering it a different sort of battle.

But she was not the sort of woman he was hunting.

The Duke of Lambley required a perfect wife. It was no different an endeavor than selecting the right butler or housekeeper. Just a matter of picking the right person for the job.

The post of duchess must be filled by a woman who had been raised in the highest echelons of society. Someone who took tea with Queen Charlotte and held the high regard of the patronesses of Almack's. Someone who looked at his ballroom not with awe, but as a small part of the sort of sprawling household she'd been trained to manage. The daughter of a peer, and utterly peerless.

He needed to marry someone above reproach, because Julian... was not. And Miss Thorne was right. He wasn't unfeeling. Julian wanted his heirs to be accepted in society. He was even prepared to turn over the proverbial new leaf if necessary to ensure his children's success.

All he asked in return was...

Perfection.

The door to the ballroom swung open. "Presenting... Lord and Lady X!"

A brightly costumed couple spilled into the

ballroom, giddy with delight at being the first through the door. Miss Thorne quickly shoved her journal back into her reticule and secured her mask.

Julian handed her a glass of champagne and gestured for her to raise it toward the new guests as was doing. He would treat Miss Thorne no differently than any other provokingly beautiful guest. It was time to play the debauched, devil-may-care host.

"To Lord and Lady X!" he called.

They each downed a glass of champagne before swirling onto the dance floor.

"Are they—" Miss Thorne began.

The ballroom door swung back open. "Presenting Lord and Lady X!"

Two more costumed revelers bounded into the room.

"Lord and Lady X!" the couple on the dance floor shouted in glee.

Miss Thorne stared. "But they—"

The door opened again.

Julian grinned at her. The party had begun.

CHAPTER 7

$\mathcal{U}$nity gazed about the ballroom. It was impossible not to get caught up in the excitement and merrymaking. New guests burst through the door every two minutes to a rousing chorus of "Lord X!" or "The Ladies X!" and enthusiastic cheers accompanied by raised glasses of champagne.

By refusing to let guests pour into his ballroom, the duke drew out the moment and made the experience seem all the more special. Each arrival was an Event and celebrated in kind. That it was also a practical matter—with the night butler confirming invitations and keeping identities anonymous on the other side—was testament to Lambley's clever mind.

Nothing he did was only the thing it seemed to be. Every decision had been contemplated and calculated and designed to evoke maximum *everything*.

This was like being on stage *with* the audience. Everyone here was part of their very own show, and they all were stars.

Unity was never an actress, but she loved the pomp of the theatre. Lambley's masquerades were the best of all worlds. The freedom to wear the costume of one's choice and play whatever role one desired without the pain of memorizing lines or dancing to someone else's choreography.

At least, so it seemed. Unity now knew how much consideration and work went into making the night look wild and spontaneous.

The lights and the decor were arranged in such a way as to draw newcomers away from the door and into one of the many entertainments. Dancing, of course. Refreshments along every wall. A promenade encircling the ballroom overhead. Private chambers just behind. Garden doors, flung open to reveal the crescent moon and stars. Couples already picking their way along stone paths or embracing on one of many secluded benches.

And Lambley was in his element. Prince of the jungle, a lion overseeing his pride, beautiful to look at and too dangerous to allow close.

He was sinfully handsome in his formal evening wear. *Informal* evening wear, Unity amended. He had not worn tails to the ball and strode about in dazzlingly white shirtsleeves paired with a crimson waistcoat and black breeches.

Shocking dishabille, by ton standards. A gentleman never showed his shirtsleeves. But the guests had not come here tonight to be respectable. Unity's deep-cut gown looked positively chaste compared to some of the costumes.

Did glimpsing a woman's ankles give an attack of the vapors? Then hie thee to the closest smelling salts because here there were men and women alike whose legs were clad only in colorful stockings or skintight pantaloons. Many a Grecian goddess dressed in little more than a bedsheet, with a slit baring a sliver of leg all the way up to her thigh.

Other men eschewed tail coats, and others avoided shirts altogether. There were several fawns and satyrs bare-chested from the waist up, and even a woman dressed as a siren with only the barest scrap of material over her breasts.

Some costumes went in the opposite direction. Extravagant peacocks—literally—with an array of tail feathers the size of an open parasol. Every sort of creature was represented, real or mythological, as well as attempts to capture the flavor of other cultures, from Egypt to India to China to Russia. There were even figures present from Britain's own history, from the famous to the infamous.

Whatever you were looking for, this was the place to find it. Whatever you wished to be, this was the place to become it.

To her surprise, no one made any snide comments or lifted their noses at the color of her skin. Lambley probably controlled that, too. Made each guest vow compliance to a list of rules so long, it truly did cover everything. Military generals and boarding school headmistresses alike would weep to be able to command their charges so thoroughly.

Best of all, Lambley made it *fun*. Every guest stepped into the ballroom with a smile upon their face that only widened as the night continued.

Next time, Unity would come as someone other than herself. Who or what, she did not yet know, but after dressing actors in costumes for so long, surely she could be more imaginative than choosing a low-cut gown and affixing a false beauty mark.

She had assumed there was no sense disguising herself because she would be the darkest-skinned guest in the ballroom, and that wasn't true either. There were already several others who shared her golden-brown hue, and a few with rich coffee coloring. She wondered if she knew them and delighted in the idea that they might be wondering the same thing about her. They could be anyone. *She* could be anyone.

The one thing all of the revelers had in common were the masks disguising their features, some from the cheeks on up and others fully covering entire visages. In some cases, she could not even be certain if the fairy tale creature she was looking at was man or woman, much less guess at their true identity. They were all too well concealed.

Everyone but Lambley, that was.

His sharp cheekbones and glittering hazel eyes were out in full force, causing many a foot to stumble and bosom to flutter.

Even though he could not know their identities—or perhaps emboldened by their anonymity—women pressed against him from all sides, shamelessly angling for a sliver of his attention.

Unity had to fight the urge to do the same.

For a man with no obvious costume, the duke played the role of indolent, careless rake with surprising aplomb. No one who glimpsed him trading cheek kisses and topping off champagne would guess how tightly strung he was beneath his *lassez-faire* hedonistic veneer.

Unity herself couldn't quite credit the full extent of her mistaken assumptions. She'd thought the challenge would be gaining admission to his private utopia. Once there, she'd work the same magic she'd used on Sampson's gaming parlor and her cousin's gentlemen's club.

Humblingly, Lambley didn't need her at all.

His masquerades were so remarkable, she ought to be paying *him* for allowing her to peep over his shoulder.

The first thing she'd decided was that doing it his way was far too much work. He was running himself into the ground by obsessing over every detail. One could not run a club this way.

Her most important lesson was not to copy him, but do the opposite.

If there was anything a lifetime lived outside the beau monde had taught her, it was that "good enough" was usually... well, *good enough.*

Perhaps it was somehow marginally better to have an odd number of fruit on each tray rather than evens, but who besides Lambley would notice or care?

In Unity's masquerade club, her refreshment tables would simply contain refreshments. Something savory, something sweet, plenty of liquid, and that would be that. She would not be measuring the distance between sandwiches or monitoring the ratio of berries to citrus.

Here in his club, she did not do much of anything. This wasn't a real partnership, or even a semi-partnership. It was an indulgence from a man who could afford to pander to every whim.

She was here until he found a bride, or she proved herself unnecessary, whichever came first. How was she supposed to seem necessary? She was surprised Lambley let his maids dust and his butlers buttle.

The moment he realized there was nothing she could offer after all, Unity would no longer be allowed within these rarefied walls.

She hoped he would let her remain for the rest of the season—there was so much she could learn!—but Unity was practical enough to know tonight could be her sole opportunity.

She drew her journal from her reticule, then shoved it back inside. She'd taken enough notes about methods and measurements. What she needed was the *feel* of the place. That was the main thing to capture. The sense of giddiness and excess, freedom and joy.

Unity gave up her position on the margins and waded into the rambunctious crowd. She could not have been labeled a wallflower—Lambley had seen to that. By encircling the ballroom with refreshment tables and provocative art, there were no empty spaces to go *be* a wallflower. Someone would appear within minutes to remark upon the delicious chocolate, or to enquire your thoughts on the nude painting of Aphrodite behind you.

The plush sofas were strategically placed as well. Not in stern lines facing forward, but cozy clumps of three or five, facing each other. To take a break from the dancing was to meet new friends somewhere else.

Someone stepped into her path.

"Have we met?" A man dressed as a Robin Redbreast—the distinct red-accented costume of the Bow Street Horse Patrol—handed her a fresh glass of champagne. Or perhaps he actually did work for the patrol and had dropped by after his shift ended.

Unity blinked. "Er..."

"I am Lord X," the Robin Redbreast said gallantly. "And you are?"

"Lady X?" Unity offered.

He beamed at her and made an impressive leg. "If this is your first masquerade, welcome! And if we've danced at every ball for the past decade, then I certainly hope we shan't break the streak tonight."

She could not help but return his easygoing smile. "It is indeed my first night. How does the duke do it?"

"Lambley?" The Robin Redbreast glanced over his shoulder. "Very, very carefully, I presume. Lambley is the definition of premeditation and tenacity. When the duke decides a thing, it will happen."

"That makes him sound more hard than fun-loving."

"He's both," said the Robin Redbreast. "Harsh and strict and relentless and more, but also the most generous soul you'll ever meet. No one multiplies money like Lambley, and no one gives it away like Lambley, either."

She stared at the Robin Redbreast. "Gives it away?"

"He has no friends in need. Not because he gets rid of the friend, but because Lambley does away with the need. He is the first to offer a loan when all seems lost, and at much better rates than the bank would ever give."

"Charging a friend interest doesn't exactly sound selfless."

The Robin Redbreast's expression was droll. "Spoken like someone who has never needed money the bank refused to give."

"No," she said softly. "I've been in situations more dire than that."

What's more, the behavior he was describing sounded awfully similar to the loans her grandfather provided in the old neighborhood. A memory Unity very much cherished, even if her grandfather's legendary generosity meant that he had given away every penny of a vast inheritance that Mother had hoped would last for generations. Grandfather cared about other people. About those whom he could help now, not later.

She would not be surprised if most of Lambley's even greater wealth was likewise spent on everyone but himself.

"You're right. Looking out for oneself does not negate looking out for others at the same time. Doesn't such generosity risk an abundance of hangers-on, rather than actual friends?"

"Again," said the Robin Redbreast, "of *course* we're hangers-on. Before you judge us too harshly for our shamelessness, I believe the duke wants it like that. Keeping us in our place is no doubt part of his strategy. He prefers to keep friends in doses he can control. Saturday nights, from ten to dawn. And we are happy to oblige. Or are you different?"

"We're not bosom friends," Unity admitted.

"But you and I could be." The Robin Redbreast held out an elbow. "Might I entice you onto the dance floor, Lady X?"

"I think you might," she said, to her surprise. "But not quite yet. I am still getting my feel for the place. Could you find me in an hour?"

"Don't forget about me," said the Robin Redbreast. "My heart will be quite shattered." He scampered off.

Unity returned her searching gaze to the Duke of Lambley.

He was somehow even more enigmatic than before. Cold and warm, closed and generous. Everyone longed to be near him, but few actually knew him.

She tried to imagine what it was like for the Robin Redbreast. To attend this party every season for years, and still not be known as anything other than Lord X. Valued enough to be given a loan if need be, irrelevant enough not to be missed between seasons.

"Handsome, ain't he?" said a swan covered in a thick blanket of white feathers.

Unity pretended she hadn't been gawking openly at her temporary employer. "Who?"

The swan rolled her eyes. "Lambley, of course. I take it you haven't had him yet."

"Had... him... I... no..."

"Figured as much. There's a different heat in a girl's eyes, once she knows what she's missing. Yours is the hunger of *wanting* to know."

"I don't... want..." Unity stammered, but it was useless. She wanted to peek inside Lamb-

ley's head and climb up his strong, tightly muscled body and the swan knew it. "It's not my
fault he's attractive," she muttered.

"He's sex in a cravat," the swan agreed. "If
you get your chance, take it."

Unity was glad her mask hid her blush.

"And then he'll be done with you." The swan
inspected her long nails. "Just one more un-
known for him to test and try and ultimately
discard once it becomes known. You'll never be
more attractive to him than the moments before
you say yes."

"I'm not planning on saying yes," Unity assured her.

"Darling, everyone in this room would say
yes. Especially those of us who know better. A
man like that... you can't help the fantasy of
being the one he wants to keep. That with you,
one night wouldn't be long enough." The swan
burst out laughing. "One night? What am I
talking about? No one has ever had him for an
entire night."

"Are you... in love with him?" Unity asked.

"Oh, no. I'm married. Although, if Lambley
were capable of love, I've no doubt the duke
could woo any maiden from her husband. Alas,
his heart is dark and shriveled. There's no room
in his rigid life for love."

"That's a cruel thing to say."

"He told me so himself." The swan shrugged.
"The only feelings I've ever seen him admit to

are displeasure and lust. He says love is for fools, and he does not suffer them."

"That sounds..."

"Cold? Heartless? He would agree."

"...*sad*," Unity finished quietly.

And perhaps inaccurate. The duke was a man who prided himself on being icy and unforgiving, yet was also known for being extraordinarily generous. He opened his home, if not his heart, and was even at this moment fetching tarts and ratafia for his guests as though he were a footman and not the lord of the manor.

What's more, he had agreed to Unity's scheme despite patently not requiring her assistance. It was like the loans, she realized. Rather than give her money as though she were a beggar, he was allowing her to "work" for her keep. Here, in the most spectacular ballroom in Mayfair.

He was helping *her*, not the other way around.

Did that sound like a coldhearted knave?

"He's the worst kind of rake," the swan warned. "The kind you know will break your heart because he tells you so before he starts. The sort of man you think you can change if you just *want* it bad enough. But there is no changing anyone, Lady X. We are all who we are."

"I won't forget," Unity vowed. "And I swear I don't wish to keep him."

"Good luck with that promise," the swan said. "Oh look, there's my husband. I promised to dance with him at least once before we select our 'amusements' for the night."

And with that, she glided through the crowd to take the arm of... the Robin Redbreast?

The charming Horse Patrol officer who had flirted with Unity was the swan's *husband?*

Good God, he might have meant for her to become his "amusement" for the evening. Unity jerked her startled eyes away. She would not be the duke's plaything or anyone else's. She was here for one reason alone: independence.

And she would let nothing stand in the way of—

"What do you think so far?" The duke. It was the Duke of Lambley. Standing right in front of her. His glittering hazel eyes concentrated solely on Unity.

"You're... it's... marvelous." She brushed a stray curl out of her face, only to realize it wasn't a curl at all, but a feather from her mask. Lambley could not see her expression, other than her mouth just beneath the bottom edge of the papier-mâché. She smiled for him. "You must know it's marvelous."

"One tries one's best," the duke demurred, but he wore no mask, and therefore his pleasure at Unity's words were plain for her to see. "Have you been propositioned yet?"

She coughed into her gloved fist.

He laughed. "It's all in good fun."

Suddenly, Unity remembered she was supposed to be a courtesan. She pretended to be put out by this proclamation. "Their offers are not serious?"

"They're very serious," Lambley corrected her. "But it's all voluntary. No one under this roof is to do anything they'd rather not, with anyone they'd rather not. Scandalous activities or otherwise. You can say no to any dance without having to sit out all the rest, and you certainly needn't go upstairs unless you wish to."

"I actually have no idea what I'd find upstairs," she reminded him. "Our tour consisted only of the ground floor."

The wickedness in his grin was unmistakable. "I can show you anything you want to see."

Unity's skin flushed and her pulse skipped. "For a 'voluntary' assignation with my host? That sounds like a dishonorable proposal, Your Grace."

"It is," he assured her. "You and I can indulge every disreputable act you can imagine, free of charge. Leave your reticule downstairs. This won't cost you a farthing."

Now she *knew* he was teasing her. Wasn't he? It was a jest, because she was the courtesan and he the one who should pay for her time. He wasn't *really* offering to take her upstairs for a thorough ravishing. Was he?

"I'll consider it," she said pertly.

To her eternal vexation, she *was* considering it, damn him. It was impossible not to. Sex in a cravat, the swan had said. *If you get your chance, take it.*

Unity could do no such thing, no matter how her quickening body felt about the sensual proposal. She needed to keep her post all season to learn everything while she still could. She could not risk being cast aside in disinterest after a ten-minute tup.

Er... thirty-minutes? An hour? How much time *would* a man like Lambley take? Would he consider his time so valuable that not a single item of clothing would be removed? Or did he treat each new conquest with the same slow, deliberate exploration that he gave everything else he touched?

He didn't care, the swan had warned. Heart of stone, incapable of love.

That was good, Unity reminded herself. She, too, was incapable of love—or at least, not permitted to indulge in such flighty nonsense until after she gained her independence. If she lay with a man, it would be because she chose him, not because she needed his money or the security he could provide her. Unity could provide those things for herself. Or would be able to. Soon.

If she could stop staring hungrily at her employer's mouth, wondering what it would be like if he kissed her.

"Perhaps after the ball," she said, "we could—"

"Everyone leaves at dawn," he said firmly. "Even you, Lady X. In fact, we should discuss your arrival time. In the future, you should not attempt early ingress. My rules are meant to be followed."

Ah, there it was. Her place.

Perhaps he *had* been serious when he offered to take her upstairs to one of the bedchambers, but his interest did not extend beyond that. She dipped an ironic curtsey. Just business, then.

Luckily, she didn't want anything more from him than that.

CHAPTER 8

Julian prowled through his crowded ballroom. He had not seen Miss Thorne since last Saturday—which was good; it meant following instructions, he had *told* her she was not allowed to arrive early, no exceptions.

Except it was now half past eleven and she wasn't here at all.

He had expected her to present herself to the night butler at five minutes to ten. Not early enough to be objectionable, but early enough to be the first through the door when the clock struck the hour.

The first through the door were a Lord and Lady X who could not be mistaken for Miss Thorne under any circumstances.

Next was a Lord X, and then another Lord and Lady X. Try as Julian might to keep half his attention on the constantly opening door, he had never given only half of his attention to his duties as host. He was needed here for this, and there for that, and the next thing he knew, his ballroom was as full as a bucket of sand, and about as easy to walk through.

Perhaps he'd frightened Miss Thorne off.

That was good, wasn't it? Julian did not *try* to be frightening, though he knew he could have that effect on certain temperaments. He would not have thought Miss Thorne to be of the swooning sort, but truly he should not be thinking of her at all. He had a party to oversee, a kingdom over which to reign, a plan underway.

The reason his ballroom was stuffed as full as the Royal Ascot with Prinny in attendance, was because his call to arms had worked. The mantel in the lavender parlor overflowed with invitations from the mothers of hopeful debutantes, each one the perfect picture of propriety.

As for Julian's ballroom... Half of the guests were people who wanted to squeeze every bit of fun out of the parties before they came to an end. The other half included significantly less respectable hopefuls convinced the Duke of Lambley would never give up his masquerades for a wife—and that they were the perfect candidate for the position.

Now that Miss Thorne had put into Julian's head that he could find a woman who was outwardly virtuous and secretly a vixen, he could settle for nothing less. Indeed, he had spent the past week carefully contemplating each of his past female guests.

First, he struck the married ones from his mental list, leaving him with half the original quantity of names. Next to go were all the women who weren't ladies. He liked them just as well, but he wasn't choosing a bride to suit himself. He was selecting the perfect duchess.

Which *could* be done. He had created the perfect masquerade, had he not?

Yes, it had taken several seasons to refine and refine again, until every glittering evening was a masterpiece. But a wife was not nearly so complicated. Besides, young ladies of the ton had trained for such roles from the moment they left the nursery.

And that was another thing to consider. Young ladies. Julian wasn't young, and had no particular interest in leg-shackling himself to some chit barely out of the schoolroom. No debutantes, then. Better yet—no one who had debuted in the past two years. Which struck several dozen more names from the list.

He could not settle for a spinster, of course. Not because of her age—the more years of life a person lived, the more interesting he or she became.

Spinsters were not to be touched for two different reasons. First, if a lady truly were perfect duchess material, some other lord would have snapped her up before she was in any danger of moldering forgotten on the shelf. And second, a perfect duchess by definition could not be some luckless unwanted wallflower, even if the loss truly was Julian's.

And third, his future heirs. He needed someone with plenty of childbearing years yet.

No spinsters and no debutantes left him with an extremely curtailed list. Julian adored extremely curtailed lists. For any conundrum, there was always a right answer. *One* right answer. One perfect duchess. The more he trimmed the list, the better.

He had thought he liked blondes well enough, but for some reason the thought did not inspire, so he struck those names from his mental list. Same for those with ghostly pale countenances. Yes, yes, porcelain white skin was perennially *à la mode*, but a chit too rigid to set down her parasol for a moment would not survive a day under this roof with Julian.

Which also meant, she must be nice, but not *too* nice, polite but not obsequious, tough enough to weather the judgments of women like the patronesses and the old dragon Lady Pettibone, but not so prickly as to invite censure upon herself or her children. Someone who—

"Is it true?" asked a skeptical voice. "Can the scandalous Duke of Lambley possibly have voluntarily stepped foot into the marriage mart?"

Julian gave his haughtiest, most forbidding stare to his good friends Lord X and Lord X— known outside these walls as the unwed Duke of

Courteland, as well as Heath Grenville, a future baron.

"No one has ever succeeded in forcing me to do something against my will," Julian said repressively.

Grenville chortled with laughter. "If I had any doubts upon the matter, that little speech would have put them to rest. By taking issue with a single word instead of answering the question, Lambley has shown his cards. I'm afraid our dear reprobate has indeed entered the marriage mart, my friend."

"Devil take you," Courteland said morosely. "I might have had a chance as the sole unmarried duke actively in search of a bride if you had stayed out of the way just a few months more."

"I *am* an attractive man," Julian said with false modesty.

The Duke of Courteland snorted. "No one cares about your handsome face. They want your title, your gold, your vast estate—"

"Trust me," Grenville said wryly. "A high percentage of the ladies in this very room are passionately interested in Lambley's handsome face. I am glad to already be married. If you knew half the things I've overheard women whisper about His Grace, the Duke of Masquerades..."

Julian was no longer attending.

He had just caught sight of a slender neck that absolutely, positively *must* belong to Miss Thorne. There were too many milling people for him to glimpse the rest of her body, and the distance stretching between them made it hard to determine the exact golden-brown of her skin, but he was certain—

"If you'll excuse me, gentlemen." Julian strode away from his friends without a word of explanation or a glance at their expressions.

There was no time.

The woman who probably, definitely, was the missing Miss Thorne was gliding toward the opposite side of the ballroom, drawing farther from Julian by the second. Already she had caught the eye of a dozen different men, all of whom started at once in her direction. If Julian did not make sufficient haste, one of them would beat him to her side and whisk her out of reach onto the dance floor.

He did not like being curt to guests, but tonight it seemed as though they were conspiring against him by putting themselves in his path to enquire or comment or compliment or —who even knew? He gave each of them a nod and promised to find them later when he was not so incredibly busy.

And then there she was.

Her attire tonight was Elizabethan. Tall red wig, low square-necked bodice, improbably small waist, impossibly wide hips, all draped in crimson velvet with white and gold taffeta. She had never looked so arresting. She—

Was not Miss Thorne. She had just turned, and in her profile—a profile that looked almost exactly like Miss Thorne's, Julian would swear to it—he could now see that the little black mole was missing from her face. It was not slathered in cosmetics or replaced by a scar. It was as though it had never existed.

Her cheekbones were different, too. He could not see them fully because of the crimson mask covering the top half of her face, but they seemed sharper tonight, as though this woman weighed a full stone lighter than curvy Miss Thorne. Even her nose seemed thinner, and the bodice of her gown fit differently.

Did she have a sister? A twin? Was that what was happening?

One of the other young bucks reached her first.

Julian had stopped moving. This was not his prey. The young buck said something that was clearly inappropriate, and the woman who was not Miss Thorne laughed—

Exactly like Miss Thorne.

He cut between the two within the space of a breath and pulled her into his side. "It *is* you."

"I... You..." She stared up at him. "How did you know?"

Miss Thorne looked shocked that he'd figured her out.

Julian was shocked he'd doubted himself at all, even for a moment.

"What happened to your mole?" he demanded.

"I never had one," she admitted. "It was putty,

colored to look like a beauty spot. Am I ugly without it?"

He ignored her teasing question and frowned. Clearly it had not been a real mole. The evidence was right in front of him. But why would she have been wearing a disguise before she'd been invited to her first masquerade?

"And your bodice?" he growled.

"Of course you'd notice that." She lowered her voice to a whisper. "I had to bind my bosom somewhat in order to fit into this gown."

All the rest of Julian's questions vanished from his mind. All that filled him now was the intense desire to be the one to unbind those plump breasts, to feel them spill into his waiting palms so that he could bring her pleasure.

"Er," said the young man who had been cut aside when Julian swooped in. "Is this an inopportune time to ask for a dance?"

Julian gave him a look so withering, it was a wonder the lad did not shrivel into a tiny speck on the spot.

"Perhaps later," the lad blurted, and scurried away without looking back.

"That was unkind," Miss Thorne chided Julian.

He lifted an eyebrow. "Did someone tell you I was kind?"

"Several people," she replied. "You really must work on keeping your bad reputation."

He glared at her.

She grinned at him.

"I'll have you know," he began, his tone frosty.

"Don't worry." She patted his arm consolingly. "They can think you generous *and* be terrified of you at the same time."

What were they talking about? Julian's ears had stopped working. And his brain. And possibly his lungs. All he could think about was her hand on his arm.

She was touching him. Surely it would be churlish not to touch her in return. He might start by flinging her extravagant red wig aside to reveal her natural glossy black curls. He wanted to feel one of those soft ringlets looped about his finger, and assure himself it was not *he* who was becoming wound around her pinkie—

Miss Thorne took her hand away.

Good. Good. He was glad for the loss.

It was ridiculous to miss her touch already. Perhaps it was not her causing this effect, but rather the simple fact of being at one of his masquerades. Heaven knew the people upstairs were engaged in far more sensual pursuits than a gentle touch upon the arm. It was the crowd's giddy comportment that clouded his emotions. He didn't even *have* emotions. He'd got rid of them years ago. This reaction was sexual, and nothing more.

He would not indulge it. *He* controlled his body, not the other way around.

"Come upstairs with me," he commanded.

It should have sounded like a command. It

did sound like a command. Sort of. A command, but also a husky, rasping plea. It would not do at all.

He cleared his throat and found his harsh, imperial tone. "Come with me."

She arched her brows. "Upstairs, Your Grace? To the rooms dedicated to unspeakable acts of pleasure? Is this to be a... business tour?"

It occurred to Julian that he did not know if she referred to the business of managing a masquerade or to her trade as a courtesan... and in his current uncomfortable state, he did not dare to ask.

He had to gain control of the situation—and himself.

"Not like that," he said gruffly. "We can save... tours... for another day. I want to show you something."

This explanation clearly did not alter her perception of the invitation, but she hooked her hand through his. "I am yours to command, my lord."

He doubted that very much.

And wanted it very much.

He led her up the staircase, but only as far as the small marble landing halfway up to the top floor. He turned her to face the crowd.

"This is the best vantage point in the ballroom."

She looked skeptical. "Better than the promenade above us?"

"It's too far away," he explained. "Up there,

you can see the ballroom from any angle, but it is more difficult to see faces. The view is obstructed by all the chandeliers. From here, I can see everyone, and they can see me."

"I've never heard 'all the chandeliers' as a negative trait before," Miss Thorne murmured. But she placed her gloved hands on the polished balustrade and gazed out over his kingdom.

He watched her in silence.

"This is your theatre box to the performance below?" she asked.

"Not quite."

The crowd caught them watching.

"To Lambley!" cheered a Lord X, thrusting his glass of champagne up high.

The rest of the crowd did the same. "To Lambley!"

"Ah, of course." Miss Thorne angled her gaze toward Julian. "This is the king's throne, and they your loyal subjects."

He did not deny it.

"But..." Her frown was hidden behind her mask, but he could hear it in her voice. "Why share your pedestal with me?"

"Any guest is welcome to climb or descend these stairs, and pause wherever they wish," he pointed out. "But you wanted to know why I do what I do. Why I care about every detail you see before you—and all of the other details that no one sees but me."

"So that masked revelers will drink to your health?"

"They wouldn't do so if they weren't enjoying themselves." His lips twitched. "Have you ever seen such a spontaneous expression of joy at Almack's?"

"I'm not allowed in Almack's," she replied blandly. "Except perhaps to clean the chamber pots."

Oof. It had been the wrong thing to say. Very wrong. Those patronesses wouldn't welcome her. They would act as though they couldn't see her. He shifted awkwardly.

Miss Thorne was not looking at him, and he was glad of it. Julian was not the sort to blush, but he was also not the sort to stick his foot so firmly into his mouth.

"I take your point," she said, rescuing him. "I've seen enough penny caricatures to know the only refreshments are weak ratafia and stale sandwiches, presided over by self-important goddesses who judge their peers more harshly than Saturn devouring his children."

Julian blinked at the esoteric reference to Roman mythology.

"People attend Almack's because they have to," Miss Thorne continued. "It's a means to an end. A way to secure their future. Whereas your guests come to your parties because they wish to. It *is* the end they're searching for. A chance to forget the future and live in this moment, in this night."

"That's exactly it," he said. "And more eloquent than I would have phrased it."

"Doubtful," she said. "You've spent hours standing right here, gazing out over the world you created. Here, you're not a king, but a deity. No doubt your mind has composed and polished the exact way it feels until each word is perfect, as sharp as the edges of your sandwiches and as colorful as the cornucopias spilling forth below."

To this, he did not respond. He was thinking perhaps it was Miss Thorne who was sharper and more colorful than previously expected.

"Or perhaps," she said, "you brought me up here to show me that it is *your* world below. Not mine. That my services are not only unwelcome, they're as superfluous as I am. That you've already achieved perfection and want for nothing."

"You're not superfluous," he murmured.

"But the rest is true?" Her voice was amused.

He considered her. "You're unfashionably direct."

"And you're unfashionably honest and surprisingly self-aware, for a peer." She tilted her head. "I expected you to deny my charge, or to throw me out for my impertinence."

"Then why risk saying it?"

"Because I'm unfashionably direct," she admitted, her eyes twinkling.

"And surprisingly honest and self-aware," he added dryly.

"See?" She pretended to place a crown atop

her head. "We've so much in common, we're practically indistinguishable."

"I'm not as pretty in a dress."

"Am I pretty?"

"You know you are."

"I know I am to *some* people," she corrected. "And *you* know I am not pleasing to all."

"I suspect you're beautiful to anyone who has ever seen you," he said. "Whether they can put up with your pert mouth and your impudent tongue, on the other hand—"

"Hurry it along, Lambley!" called one of the revelers. "I've got ten quid on you kissing her before midnight, not jawing the poor girl to sleep!"

Miss Thorne looked startled. "They're not... *really* wagering on..."

Julian could not allow his revelers to see him treating Miss Thorne differently than any other woman. They might think it meant she affected him in some way. That she threw him off balance. Julian was never off balance. He was in control of himself and this moment, and would give his guests the performance they expected and desired.

"I don't jaw," Julian informed his audience coldly. "I am a man of few words... and stealing high-stakes kisses."

He pulled Miss Thorne into his arms.

"What are you doing?" she stammered. But she did not resist. Her hands on his upper arms clutched him tight, rather than pull away.

"Pleasing the crowd." He lowered his lips to a mere breath above hers. "May I kiss you, Lady X, for the sake of theatre?"

"Only for theatre's sake," she repeated, the words breathless. "Don't fool yourself into thinking I—"

He covered her mouth with his.

Her tongue found his at once. His hands followed the curve of her spine to the small of her back and pressed her closer to him. Her hands twisted in his hair, destroying his perfectly starched high collar. He had never cared less about being fashionable than in that moment.

The crowd cheered. Glasses clinked. The wager was won.

Julian did not pull his lips from Miss Thorne's. He could barely hear the crowd over the thundering of his heart. All he could feel was satin over soft curves. *Bound* curves that he wished to unbind.

All he could smell was the faint almond-and-vanilla scent of her hair. All he could taste was the champagne on her tongue. All he wanted was to scoop her up into his arms and charge up the stairs to the closest bedchamber, whereupon he would finally find—

Control. He was out of control. His heart was beating wildly, his thoughts in disarray, and he had completely forgotten whatever point he'd thought he was trying to make.

He broke the kiss at once, snapping his spine

to a kingly height in order to gaze coolly at the crowd.

"To Lambley and Lady X!" they cried, raising their bubbling champagne glasses high until the ballroom itself glittered like a chandelier.

"If you'll excuse me," Julian said, and descended his royal steps to melt into the crowd without risking any more kisses.

He wanted to stop. To turn and look at Miss Thorne. To run back up the steps and toss her over his shoulder without slowing until they were naked and sweating.

But *he* was in control, not his libido. Besides, Miss Thorne was not a duchess candidate. If she tempted him to forget himself, he should stay clear of casual dalliances as well.

Perhaps break all contact with her.

He strode toward Heath Grenville, drawing him aside. "I have a job for you."

"Name it," Grenville replied without hesitation.

The future baron was known throughout the ton as a solver of problems. He could not be taxed with the conundrum of Julian's suddenly wavering self-control, but he could investigate another matter for him.

Julian kept his voice low. "Find out who she is."

"Don't you know?" Grenville answered in obvious surprise.

"I know her name," Julian said. "The night

butler will give it to you when you are out of range from eager ears."

Grenville nodded. "Understood. What do you want me to find out?"

Julian pushed away all thoughts of the softness of her body, the heat of her kiss. He almost hadn't recognized her tonight. Not because she was wearing an Elizabethan costume, but because she wasn't wearing her *usual* disguise. Something was not right.

He found it difficult to trust others under the best of circumstances. He would not allow himself to be gammoned because of a pretty face.

"Start with whether that's her real name," he said. "And then find out everything you can. If she has an ulterior motive, I need to know it. If she has a secret, uncover it. I want to know everything."

"I'll need a little time."

"You'll be compensated handsomely for speed."

"Very well." Grenville inclined his head and disappeared into the night butler's vestibule to speak to Fairfax.

Only then did Julian allow his gaze to travel back to the marble staircase.

She was gone.

CHAPTER 9

The warm spring sun fell on the back of Unity's bare neck as she stepped off of the pavement and into a bustling outdoor market. Vendors surrounded her, some shouting in front of fruit or vegetable stands, and others threading through the crowd, hawking posies or oysters from baskets like the one Unity carried.

Hers was empty, just like her larder. Between the long days at the theatre and the long night at the duke's masquerades, she'd been too busy to think of much else. This morning when she broke her fast with her last egg and the final hunk of stale bread, she knew she could escape the real world no longer.

But, oh, how she yearned to! She wished she were shopping not for her small shelf in her apartment's shared pantry, but for the future masquerade-themed assembly rooms she would one day open.

She was tired of being frugal and conservative and quiet. Everyone complimented her on being so resourceful, on finding a way when there was none, on turning scraps into something more. But who wanted to live like that?

"Soon," she murmured as she threaded her way through the crowd.

Was that true? She hoped so. The dream of not just being financially secure, but the owner of a thriving establishment she could be proud of had filled her every thought for so long, and had given her much-needed hope on countless bleak days. It was her favorite fantasy to dream about, the picture she painted in her mind at every opportunity—

Or, at least, it *had* been.

It still was! It definitely still was. It was just... A certain duke had begun to creep into her thoughts more and more. Pah. He was nothing more than a temporary distraction. A distraction who had *kissed* her. There could be nothing more distracting than that!

And their embrace was just theatre. He'd walked away from their kiss—walked away from *her*—like an actor hanging up his wig after a performance.

Unity should know. She'd seen it thousands of times. Ordinary people became Hamlet or Joan of Arc for three hours but returned to their true selves as soon as the curtains closed.

Lambley played two roles: Magnanimous Host and Irresistible Rake. She'd merely been caught at the intersection last night on the stairs. An accident of proximity. The audience demanded a kiss, and so he had kissed her.

No—he had kissed Lady X, not Unity. A nameless, faceless figment of the crowd's collective imagination. They hadn't wanted him to kiss *her*. They didn't know or care who the person was beneath the mask. They just wanted a show. It wasn't personal.

And she was a professional, too, was she not?

Unity balanced her basket on her hip in order to dig a small journal out of her reticule. The coins she had earned from her time at the masquerade clinked in the bottom as she turned to a fresh page in her book.

With a nub of pencil, she jotted down, *Determine what show my audience wants and give it to them.* A valuable lesson. Her crowd would differ significantly from the duke's, but the general principle remained the same.

Her lips quirked. Oh, how the rigid Duke of Lambley would rankle if he knew Unity thought him a glorified theatre manager!

He plied his trade on Grosvenor Square rather than Drury Lane, but he alone controlled the set, the casting, the script, and the curtain call. A grand performance every Saturday from ten to six, available only to ticket holders. Please wait at the entrance for the usher to admit you...or to show you out.

She snickered to herself as she added rhubarb and elderflower to her basket and paid the vendors. If she were an artist, how might she design a playbill advertising his masquerades? The duke didn't just manage the production—he was also the star.

Perhaps the illustration should be of his stern countenance in profile. A forbidding silhouette, to show that this was a serious, intellectual drama, the sort people loved to brag about having attended, in order to prove how sophisticated they were. Or perhaps the playbill should depict the duke in footlights upon the stage, showered in a deluge of falling roses, to highlight the themes of romance and desire. That was universal, wasn't it? Or perhaps a better idea—

She turned from the chicory vendor and twitched to a halt.

He was here. *Here.*

Not ten feet from her, haggling over spring onions.

No, no, he couldn't be *haggling*. Surely, he wasn't here at all, and last night's kiss had turned Unity temporarily mad.

He must have an entire army of maids who came to market carrying rulers and scales, ensuring every gooseberry conformed to exacting standards of perfection before it was allowed into a perfectly engineered basket, to be carried into an equally perfect scullery.

She watched as he tossed a silver crown to the vendor. Enough coin to buy an oxcart of onions. He did not wait for his change.

Definitely not haggling.

And definitely the Duke of Lambley.

He looked handsome and out-of-place in a well-cut dark blue coat with twin columns of gold buttons, a frothy white neckcloth above a black silk waistcoat, spotless tawny buckskins clinging to powerful thighs, and shiny black Hessian boots, complete with a jaunty tassel just below each knee.

The duke turned away from a particularly insistent flower girl, now holding a newly acquired posy, and met Unity's amused gaze. His hazel eyes widened for only a moment before he quickly schooled his features into their usual impassive mask of arrogance and ennui.

Unity wasn't fooled for a second.

He was standing in a *market*. And had just been manipulated by a ten-year-old into buying flowers he didn't want or need. She sauntered up to him without bothering to school her expression.

"Shopping for your next party?" she asked with faux politeness.

"If you must know," he answered coldly, "indeed I am."

She wished she could raise a single eyebrow. "Isn't that a task usually reserved for underlings and dogsbodies?"

The duke had no problem arching a lonesome brow. "A curious statement, considering *you're* here shopping as well."

"I have no servants," she pointed out dryly.

She should not have done. A frown of confusion marred his handsome face.

To him, she was not Unity Thorne, costume and cosmetics worker, but rather a fashionable courtesan he had never seen wearing anything but a fancy ball gown.

Until today.

She had carefully constructed the impression that she was a demimondaine of the calibre that certainly would have a respectable quantity of servants to attend her every need, only to pop up in the middle of a market wearing a yellow day dress with the elbows worn thin and a straw bonnet whose edges had begun to fray.

"Are you in disguise?" he said doubtfully.

"Some of us don't limit our role-playing to one night per week," she replied. There. That was vague and could be interpreted in many different ways. She attempted to guide the conversation in a different direction. "You seem as surprised to see me as I was to see you."

"I was just thinking about you and there you were," he murmured.

She expected him to wince or to color or to otherwise indicate that he regretted speaking without thinking.

Instead, his gaze held hers without flinching.

Of course the Duke of Lambley would not speak without thinking. He had been thinking about her, and now they both knew it. But why had he told her? Because she was "Miss Thorne, Courtesan"?

No, that was not it. Another man might have been interested in procuring a saucy mistress, but Lambley's attention infamously waned before dawn, and the tryst never repeated.

Nor had he any need to pay for such encounters. His home filled with willing bodies every week. He had only to crook his finger at a woman, and she was his for the taking. Had Unity not proved as much herself, by kissing him with abandon in front of hundreds of watching eyes?

But she would not be intimidated. She was almost his equal in one sense, whether he believed it or not. Soon-to-be proprietress of the newest masquerade establishment on everyone's lips.

Well, everyone in her circles.

"I was thinking about you, too," she replied, as though the topic were no more consequential than cabbages and watercress. "And then there you were."

"Specifically," he said, "I was thinking about our kiss."

Well.

"Specifically," she replied, "I haven't stopped thinking of it."

There. She waited for him to say that it was a mistake. Or to proposition her to one night of torrid passion, followed immediately by never seeing each other again.

He said nothing of the sort. Just watched her, with his forbidding, carved-marble countenance. His eyes, however, were not hard at all. They gazed at her with the same hunger she'd glimpsed last night, right before his mouth claimed hers.

"Are you just finishing up?" he asked.

She shook her head. "Just starting."

"Then I shall accompany you." He tugged her basket from her suddenly weak fingers and looped the handle over his strong forearm.

"Oh," she managed weakly. "There's no need to—"

"Do you want to hold the posy, or shall I place it in the basket?"

"You didn't buy the flowers for me," she stammered.

"And yet," he replied, "I find it is you whom I wish to give them to."

Heat rushed her cheeks. "B-basket."

There was no way she could stroll casually about the market with a posy from the duke clutched in her sweaty, trembling fist. She was no one, but he was recognizable from dozens of caricatures. He *knew* he could be recognized, standing here, sparring with *her*. And he cared not one whit what the gossips would have to say. The Duke of Lambley did as he wished, and what he wanted in this heady, inexplicable moment, was to give a posy to Unity.

He dropped the flowers inside her basket.

For a brief, mad moment, she imagined he might offer her his free arm.

He did nothing of the sort.

Her cheeks flushed hotter, and she cut her gaze away as she fell into step beside him. Of course he could not offer his arm. Who did she think she was, a princess? She should count herself flattered that he condescended to carry her basket.

She *was* flattered, damn him. And embarrassed that she'd thought for even a moment that it might mean anything more than a courtly gentleman's act of kindness. Their worlds did not intersect outside of his anonymous masquerades.

In fact, he wouldn't dare to stroll next to her if she were one of his upper-class set. Being alone with a debutante was scandalous enough to send him to the altar, whether he liked it or not.

But with her, such proximity did not signify. Unity did not count. It was like being alone with a servant in one's employ.

She *was* in his employ, she realized grimly. That was exactly the situation. Working for him was her idea. What was she complaining about? She had got her way. Huzzah.

Besides, they weren't really alone. The market swarmed with people. And a lord like Lambley probably had a footman or twelve following at a discreet distance at all times.

She should just enjoy this unexpected moment for what it was, and forget about all it was not and could never be.

"I enjoyed your party," she said casually, as

she inspected a box of parsnips. "For a reclusive misanthrope, you certainly surround yourself with a prodigious number of people."

He slanted her a quelling glare. "I didn't say I liked them."

"You didn't have to." She dropped her parsnips into the basket. "You wouldn't care so much about your guests' enjoyment if you didn't also care about your guests."

He looked adorably disgruntled. "Clearly you mistake what it means to be a gentleman, who must do as is right, regardless of his feelings on the matter."

"Mm-hm."

Clearly the Duke of Lambley was as soft on the inside as he was hard on the outside. A puff pasty, whose crusty exterior hid nothing more alarming than warm, gooey sweetness. And he didn't even realize it.

She paused before a stand of carrots.

"Select whatever you like," commanded the duke. "I'll have it sent to your home."

"You'll do nothing of the sort." She lifted her chin to glare at him. "I don't want or need your charity."

The opposite. She wanted to prove herself capable. Prove herself worthy. To him, and to herself, and to the world.

"As the lady wishes," he said without argument, in a tone that might have been accompanied by a careless shrug if the Perfect

Gentleman were not so great a personage as a duke.

She forced her attention to the carrots, lest she stare at him in consternation all day.

The night butler was right. Lambley was wealthy and privileged and thought he knew best, and he tried to use all of that to help others.

He was assertive, but not demanding. He'd informed her of his plan rather than ask her opinion of it, but when she declined his offer, he immediately respected her decision with no further questions or arguments to sway her mind.

His mystified expression indicated he had no idea *why* she would turn down his money—perhaps no one else ever had—but he made no attempt to encroach upon her autonomy.

That, or he was too consumed trying to control his own life to bother unnecessarily with hers.

"What?" he demanded.

She widened her eyes at him. "I was thinking about your night butler."

"He's married," Lambley said flatly.

She ignored this. "Mr. Fairfax said you gave him that position without him asking for it. That it hadn't even occurred to him you might be in the market for such a thing."

"He's married *and* he lacks imagination."

"He says you're a very good friend."

Lambley grunted and flicked a hand toward the carrots. "Are you buying any of these or not?"

She tried not to smile. "Are you actively trying to give the impression you do not work well with others?"

He looked aghast. "Why would I want to work with others?"

Her laugh caught in her throat when she realized he wasn't playing along with her jest, but deadly serious.

"Now I know you're teasing," she said uncertainly. One could not rule from on high all of the time, unless one was a king... or perhaps a duke? "Surely there are people not in your employ whom you rely on, someone who would make a good partner, or part of a... team..."

He looked more horrified at each word she spoke.

"*I* am all the team I need." His tone brooked no argument.

Unity turned back to the carrots.

She understood wanting to prove oneself. She was in the midst of attempting that very thing. But she didn't wish to be lonesome forever. She had worked well with Sampson at his gambling den. She was one small part of a large team that put on intricate performances at the theatre. Neither was the future she longed for, but her life would not be richer for locking herself away.

Lambley had *said* she could be his temporary assistant, but he hadn't meant it. He intended to let her trail behind him, then toss a pile of sovereigns at her and send her on her way without ever truly considering her opinions or potential value.

He was making a mistake.

She would teach him. Unity was determined not just to prove herself, but to prove him wrong. To contribute, to help. She could be useful... if he allowed her to try.

"What if," she said slowly, "we changed the menu a tiny bit—"

"No."

"Just for one night—"

"No."

"Just one item—"

"No."

"You don't even know what I'm proposing we change it *to*," she burst out.

He raised his brows. "It doesn't matter. It's not your party."

"Give me my basket back," she muttered.

He smiled. "No."

She tossed far more carrots than she needed inside just to make the basket heavier. "What's the worst that could happen?"

"I will not change something that is good for something that might be less so."

"'Might,'" she pounced. "Then you admit it also might be *better*. Let's start with something simple. Why are you so committed to maintaining the status quo of your little triangle sandwiches?"

"I have tested the matter extensively. They are of a perfect size to easily consume in three bites. Any larger, and sandwich remnants litter the trays, or one risks the filling sliding out. Any smaller, and guests have to queue more often to refill their plates. What is your vendetta against my perfect sandwiches?"

"It's not the sandwiches," she said. "I believe you when you say every item in your home is the best possible version of that item in the entire world, at least insofar as you've been able to make it."

"Then what is your point?"

"Variety is my point. Surprise is my point. New experiences are my point. Listening to outside opinions is my point. Maybe other people's suggestions are better. Maybe they're not. If things don't go to plan, it's all right."

He gave her a forbidding gaze. "*My* plans always go exactly as intended."

"So you planned to run into me today and argue from the turnips to the asparagus?"

His scowl deepened.

"All right," she said. "I can compromise."

"I cannot."

She pretended not to have heard him. "What if, next Saturday, we meet an hour early to sample new items that we both already know you fully intend to veto?"

He stared at her for a long moment, his gaze inscrutable. "As long as you understand that's precisely what will happen. And I shall pay for the ingredients."

She reached for the basket. "I told you, I—"

"No arguments. It is now an entertaining expense that I must cover, as host of the party."

"Hogwash," she said. "You already know you're going to reject all of my suggestions, therefore it has nothing to do with your party at all. You just want to win."

He grinned at her. "I always win."

Except he hadn't. He had let *her* take this round.

They both knew she could not force him to taste potential new dishes. He had agreed because... oh, who knew how his mind worked? Either he secretly enjoyed letting her take charge, or her queries had made him fear she'd think of something he hadn't. He'd feel honor-bound to exhaustively test all possibilities.

Which made Unity honor-bound... to let him. She schooled her features into a mask of innocence to hide a spark of devilry. In Act One, Lambley was used to getting his way. He thought he'd ended the matter by condescending to taste a creation he'd already dismissed out of hand.

But Act Two was just beginning.

CHAPTER 10

"Shall we continue with black currants?" Unity did not wait for an answer, but continued on toward the first row of fruit stands.

She kept her eyes wide and her expression rapt as she listened to a long, boring lecture about which currants were fit for a ducal kitchen. She nodded sagely at each carefully researched conclusion.

When at last he finished his speech, he lifted his brows expectantly.

She reached out, plucked two plump berries at random, popped one into her mouth, and tossed the other at him.

He caught it out of reflex.

It was Unity's turn to raise her brows expectantly.

A muscle worked at the duke's temple. Politeness dictated he not be rude to a woman, nor offend the fawning vendor. With obvious ill temper, he placed the berry into his mouth and made a tight-lipped smile at the supplier as he chewed.

"You're right," Unity said at once, handing the vendor a penny for his troubles. "Not these. Let's try the raspberries."

She set off for the next stand.

Lambley caught up as soon as he'd retrieved Unity's penny and purchased a pint of delightfully imperfect currants at no doubt an exorbitant price.

He was opening his mouth to scold her when he arrived.

"Is there an empirical method to determining the optimal raspberry?" she asked before he could get a word out.

His lips tightened only briefly. Of course there was a best method, which he had devised himself after much experimentation, and which he now enunciated in exhaustive detail.

"Mm-hm," Unity said when he finished, and plucked two crimson berries at random from the cart. One for her, one tossed at him.

By the time they reached the blackberries, Lambley was on to her. He was also in possession of several quarts of imperfect fruit.

By the time they reached the elderberries, he'd ceased explaining his detailed berry-judging methodology, and switched to lecturing about a fictional law that included never allowing women in yellow dresses to opine on his kitchens, followed by lamenting the inferior berry-choosing capabilities of insolent young women whose name began with the letter U.

By the time they reached the strawberries, Unity was laughing too hard to listen to his increasingly dramatic speeches, and Lambley was trying too hard *not* to laugh to say anything coherent or truly disdainful.

Unity popped a strawberry into his mouth before he could get going on another tangent.

The duke's eyes widened at this impertinence, but since his mouth was too full to scold her properly, he retaliated by lifting a strawberry from the cart and placing it between *her* lips instead.

Her mouth exploded with flavor. He had, of course, selected a bright red berry ripe enough to be sweet and firm enough to have a hint of tartness to balance out the flavor.

"That's a good strawberry," she was forced to admit.

The duke gasped in faux outrage. "You *doubted* my strawberry-selection capabilities? After all we've been through together on this interminable market escapade, you possess the unthinkable affrontery to—"

She dragged him to the cherry cart.

Their silly, delicious berry war was more fun than she'd ever imagined having with the Duke of Lambley. He took his masquerades so seriously, she hadn't been certain the man was even capable of *fun*. But here they were, teasing each other and feeding each other and arguing passionately over meaningless details that neither of them cared about, because they were no longer in this market to buy food. They were still here because they were enjoying each other.

Only when not a single berry more would fit into her overflowing basket did they declare themselves defeated, and made their way out of the market to the queue of carriages lined along the street.

"Which one is yours?" he asked.

A real courtesan of the rank Unity was pretending to belong to would have a coach-and-four at her disposal.

"I walked," she admitted, and hoped he merely thought her eccentric. "I'll summon a hackney—"

"Nonsense. My coach is right here."

She'd noticed it at once, of course. It was impossible not to. The distinctive coat of arms painted upon the door, the matched pair of tall, regal... uh... Unity didn't know enough about horses to begin to guess their breed, but even to her ignorant eye, these two were the finest pair in the queue.

A blue-and-gold liveried footman opened the door for them, but it was Lambley who handed her up and into the luxurious interior.

Unity had never been inside a conveyance half so fine, but when her temporary arrangement with Lambley ended, it would not be his plush carriage or his gilded ballroom that she missed the most.

It would be the hour she'd spent with him today at the market.

"To where shall I instruct the coachman?" he asked.

Unity hesitated. She could not give the direction of her tiny room in a shared apartment and have him believe anyone of his class would visit such mean lodgings. Not only did she need to keep the charade intact, a vexing part of her also could not bear for him to think less of her because of her address and significantly lower station than High Class Courtesan.

She gave him her cousin's address instead.

At this time in the afternoon, Roger would be at his club already. She hadn't lived in his home since the day he'd thrown her out, but the servants still remembered her. They would allow her in the front door, and then she could walk through to the back and continue home down the alleys. She'd give the staff a few quarts of fruit to share amongst themselves for their trouble.

The walk home would be longer, but the small deception would be worth it. She didn't want to jeopardize her chance at future moments like these with Lambley.

Not when he was looking at her as though he had found the perfect berry, ripe for the tasting.

They were no longer speaking. The easy banter of the marketplace had been replaced by a tension thick as custard and just as tempting. Lambley's leonine eyes watched her as though he were keeping himself tethered on his side of the carriage out of sheer force of will.

She wished he wouldn't.

The kiss they had shared had been heavenly. It had also been public. The knowledge so many eyes were upon her had distracted her from being fully able to enjoy the moment.

No eyes were upon them now. If he wanted to kiss her again, he could.

But he did not.

Perhaps she was not as winsome without an audience. His only playtime was Saturday nights from ten to six, with the rest of the week devoted to the serious business of wife-hunting. No—*duchess* hunting.

Unity would not be cast in the role. She was the wrong class, wrong color, wrong everything.

But she didn't want to be anyone's wife. Unity had her own plans. What she wanted at the moment was to be a woman the duke had welcomed into his embrace because he wished to. Because he chose to.

She needed to know if the kiss they'd shared had been real, or a trifling bit of showmanship undertaken to please his audience.

"Thank you for the fruit," she murmured.

He scoffed. "I don't care about the fruit."

"I have never seen someone care more deeply about fruit than the Duke of Lambley in front of a gooseberry cart."

"Fruit is no less important than anything else."

And *that* was what made him all the more intriguing as a lover. He would not be content with a fumble in the dark. He would want to know the woman in his arms. Every inch. Her skin, her scent, her moans, her taste. He would not be a careless lover, interested only in his own pleasure. He would find all the secret places and not rest until he brought—

He leaned forward, his voice husky, his eyes hot on hers. "Stop me."

"No." She grabbed his lapels and pulled him forward, even as his mouth crashed over hers.

This time, he did not smell of rich cologne and taste of even more expensive champagne. His mouth tasted tart and sweet, the memory of every playful argument they had shared still lingering on their tongues.

His hands cupped her face, his fingers cradling her gently while his tongue teased and took, ravishing her and romancing her all at once.

This was not a kiss for an audience. This was the kiss *he* wanted to take, the kiss he wanted to *give*.

To her.

Unity met him parry for parry, kiss for kiss. She disentangled her hands from his lapels only to slide her hungry fingers beneath them, seeking the warmth of his hard, muscled body and the insistent beat of his heart against her palm.

His waistcoat was embroidered silk. Soft and

slippery in comparison to the rough heat coiled within him. He felt like strength and power, danger and wealth. Wound far too tight beneath a thin veneer of control. He kissed her as though he were seconds away from rending both their garments to the floor of the carriage.

If he did so, she would fall down upon them and pull him to her to finish what they started, right here on the floor.

"We've arrived, Your Grace." The coach came to a sudden stop.

Unity jerked her fingers out of the duke's coat and smoothed his hopelessly wrinkled lapels.

He still held her face, his lips brushing against hers one last time before drawing just far enough away to meet each other's eyes.

"We must stop this once I choose my duchess."

That was a cold dash of water.

"Or when *I* wish to stop." She pulled out of his reach. "Don't be so arrogant as to assume I— wait. Do you mean to imply the lord of masquerades won't so much as kiss another person once he's betrothed?"

Lambley shrugged as if her shock held no merit. "I shan't kiss anyone but my bride from the moment I've ascertained who it will be."

Unity blinked. Not only was that not how the ton tended to operate, the duke's parties implied a rather flexible understanding of traditional marital vows.

"Your monogamy starts even before *she* knows she's your duchess?"

"*I* will know."

It was like the fruit and the champagne towers and the careful arrangement of chairs. Once Lambley decided on a path, nothing would sway him—or tempt him. Not even a house full of scantily clad guests eager for a tryst upstairs.

His perfect future duchess would want for nothing. The duke would be hers. Body and soul.

Even though it was foolish, Unity could not help but wonder what it might be like to have someone feel that way about her.

CHAPTER 11

*J*ulian rose from his escritoire when Heath Grenville entered the study for their scheduled appointment. The duke's first impulse was to spring on his guest and demand to know everything Grenville had uncovered about Miss Thorne.

Instead, he offered his friend a glass of port from the sideboard.

"Any news?" he allowed himself to ask once they were comfortably ensconced in a pair of armchairs. Night had fallen already.

Grenville reached into an inner pocket of his frock coat and handed Julian a folded sheet of parchment. "Broad strokes at this time. I'm working on filling in the details."

Julian tucked the report into his own inner pocket and handed Grenville a different scrap of paper. "I dropped her off at this address yesterday. An unusual direction for a courtesan. See what you can find out."

Grenville glanced at the writing and smiled. "You'll find the answer already in your report. This residence belongs to her first cousin, a Mr. Roger Thorne."

Julian's eyebrows rose. "A courtesan who lives with a male cousin? The house and surroundings seemed respectable. Could Mr. Thorne not provide for his relative in some other manner?"

"Perhaps she, like you, chooses to be 'disreputable,'" Grenville chided Julian. "You were not scandalized by her profession until it occurred to you she might not need to pursue it."

"I'm not scandalized," Julian muttered.

Miss Thorne could do as she pleased. His disinclination to imagine her lying with other gentlemen was of absolutely no significance whatsoever.

"For the record," Grenville continued, "she has not lived at that address in some years."

"What?" Julian sat up with a start. "Why would she give me a false address?"

"Because she doesn't want you to know her real one?" Grenville asked innocently.

Julian scowled at him. "What is her current address?"

"I'm investigating," Grenville assured him.

"It makes no sense." Julian swirled his port without sipping it. "Courtesans entertain at their homes. Why not share its location with me?"

"Why would she need to?" Grenville countered. "Your reputation for never repeating romantic encounters is universally known. Unless your habits have changed?"

"I never change."

He had kissed her twice, but he did not yet need to stop. The rule was never to repeat *love-making* with the same individual. No exceptions.

"I should've known you'd never relax a rule," Grenville said wryly. "Or... relax."

"I relax!" Julian protested.

This assertion was not, normally, the case. However, there was no better way to describe his encounter with Miss Thorne at the market than an extraordinary episode of unplanned relaxing.

"Tell me about the cousin," he ordered. "When did she cease to live with him?"

"Some years after he opened a gentlemen's club. Have you heard of the Wit & Whistle?"

Julian frowned. "Maybe I did, once."

"That is the way of it. The Wit & Whistle was ignored and unfrequented for years. It then briefly became quite popular, before fading back into oblivion."

Julian shrugged. "I pay no attention to such things. I am not a member of any club."

"Of course not. You confine all your vices to the six hour period of your masquerade."

"Eight hours," Julian muttered.

Grenville grinned at him, making it obvious he'd purposefully provoked Julian into correcting the precise duration of his scheduled weekly amusement, rather than address the implication he rarely left his home.

"Will you be visiting the cousin's club?" Grenville asked.

"No," Julian responded.

He wasn't reclusive... exactly. That was a side effect, not the aim. He simply wished to be in complete control of everything and everyone in his orbit.

Which, yes, did imply he would rather go through the expense and effort of hosting and managing his own parties than he was likely to trust someone else's plans or judgment.

"There's no reason to visit the Wit & Whistle," he informed Grenville. "Miss Thorne wouldn't be present at a gentlemen's club."

"First," said Grenville, "you may be unaware that while such exclusive clubs are not open to *ladies*, it is not at all unusual to discover the presence of demimondaines within their hallowed walls."

Julian drained his port rather than respond. He was doing his very best not to think about Miss Thorne in the arms of other men, at the Wit & Whistle or anywhere.

And he refused to contemplate the potential reasons for his discomfort.

"Second," Grenville continued, "the doors of this particular club would open to her without hesitation. It appears Miss Thorne was the one managing the Wit & Whistle during its rise and peak of popularity."

"Miss Thorne... ran a gentlemen's club?"

"Not just ran," Grenville reminded him. "Turned it profitable."

Julian stared at him.

"I know what you're thinking." Grenville's eyes twinkled. "How unseemly of the lower classes to dabble in trade."

This was a private jest between them. Grenville was heir to a barony, yet solved the ton's indelicate situations in exchange for coin. Julian had no need for others' money, but was often teased that he worked more hours than his own servants.

"She created a profitable gentlemen's club," he repeated, "...and then became a courtesan?"

"The investigation is ongoing," Grenville replied noncommittally.

Julian tightened his jaw.

Grenville was doing his best. His forte was *keeping* secrets, not uncovering them. The ton employed him to bury their little details before they became big scandals.

Julian didn't give a fig about idle gossip. He wasn't the least bit reputable, and until he'd begun the duchess hunt, such things never caused him concern. But now that he *was* on the market...

"What do you think?" he asked. "Am I too scandalous to secure an impeccable bride?"

"You're pretty peccable," Grenville admitted. "For as long as you continue to throw masquerades in the manner in which you currently host them, you will continue to receive understandable censure."

"Ninety-nine percent of my guests have never ventured upstairs," Julian pointed out. "Most attend for the luxuries on display and the thrill of being scandal adjacent. And none are ever invited into my private quarters."

"That is as may be," Grenville said. "But what has it to do with Miss Thorne?"

"Nothing," Julian said. "Why would my personal life have anything to do with Miss Thorne?"

"Mm," said Grenville. "I see. Well, if you're ever serious about mending your infamous reputation, let me know and I shall do my utmost to assist you. In the meantime, I shall carry on with the current, completely-unrelated-to-your-bride-hunt project."

"Do that," Julian growled.

Unperturbed, Grenville set his empty glass on a side table and rose to his feet. "I shall send a note when I have something further to report."

Once his friend had taken his leave, Julian moved to stare moodily out through the window. It would be too dark to see anything but his own reflection, had the footmen not lit the path with dozens of lanterns in anticipation of tonight's masquerade.

The carriages had not yet begun to queue. It was only nine o'clock.

He removed the report from his pocket and scanned its contents, then read it again, slower the second time. It contained marginally more detail than uncovered in their conversation, most of which centered about the club and the cousin.

Julian didn't care about that. He wanted to know more about Miss Thorne. She was a conundrum. If he'd thought a modicum of information would sate his appetite, the opposite had occurred. Each new detail begat more questions.

He did have one answer. It seemed that her offer of assistance had not only been in earnest... she had reason to believe herself capable of fulfilling that duty.

But Julian's masquerades were not some ill-run, no-name club of little standing. To be clear, putting that to rights was indeed a feat—and one her cousin was apparently incapable of achieving—but improving something terrible was far easier than improving something that had already been polished to perfection.

He filed the report in a drawer and then bade his brain to cease thinking about Miss Thorne.

It didn't work.

Julian was not thinking about her family situation or her managerial acumen, but rather the kisses they'd shared in his carriage. He hadn't meant to kiss her. In fact, he'd decided very firmly *not* to.

And then she was right in front of him, being beautiful and maddening and irresistible, and the next thing he knew, the line had gone from "never again" to "we'll part once I've chosen a bride."

He hadn't wanted to stop. He would've driven about the city for hours, just to keep on kissing her. If she *would* have given her true address, if she *would* have invited him inside...

Oh, who was he kidding? Julian had been so discombobulated by their encounter in the market, he'd forgotten to purchase the items he'd traveled there to select in the first place. Of *course* he would have gone upstairs with Miss Thorne and engaged in any activity she wished.

And of course she would have been aware of his reputation for refusing second encounters. She might have thought that indulging the itch they both longed to scratch would have resulted in losing his interest altogether.

Which was indeed what would have happened. Wouldn't it?

Heaven knew he wasn't *smitten* with her. He was incapable of emotions, soft or otherwise. These fireworks were just chemistry. His attention would wander any day now. It was a miracle she'd distracted him for this long. He wouldn't go on like this *forever*.

He was busy. Very busy.

Julian arranged himself at his escritoire and reached for the correspondence he'd been attending to before Grenville arrived.

Barnaby appeared in the doorway.

"Pardon the intrusion, Your Grace," said the butler. "Miss Thorne is here to—"

Julian leapt to his feet. "Where did you put her?"

"The green parlor, Your Grace. As you requested."

Julian strode down the corridor, slowing only when the parlor door came into view, so that he could saunter through the door in a sedate and disaffected manner. Because he was sedate and disaffected.

Mostly.

Maybe.

Her eyes lit up when she saw him. His blood pulsed faster. Rather than curtsey—or kiss him —she deposited a square, cloth-covered basket in his hands.

"What is this?"

She swept the scrap of linen from the short, squat basket with all the flair of a magician unveiling a stunning metamorphosis.

"Biscuits!" Her smile lit her face and her brown eyes sparkled with amusement. "In a style that you don't offer at your masquerades."

"Nor will I," he said coldly.

The cursed things smelled absolutely delicious.

Miss Thorne plopped onto his bespoke Chippendale sofa as though it had been made for comfort rather than aesthetics. She patted the cushion beside her as if she were the hostess and he the guest she was graciously allowing into her parlor.

Stiffly, he placed the basket on the hand-carved tea table before the sofa and took his seat beside her. Not because the Duke of Lambley followed anyone else's orders, but because it was the most convenient seat from which to share fresh-baked biscuits.

...and efficient proximity in the event he decided to haul her into his lap and kiss her.

"Shortbread," she informed him.

Yes, he could see that it was shortbread.

Shortbread was the sort of treat one might find in a country house in Scotland. Not the sort of confection one might expect in a ducal ballroom where exquisite refreshments were presided over by a talented team of French chefs.

"They're circles," said Miss Thorne.

"I see that." He raised his brows. "Is there a reason for the round shape?"

She beamed at him as though she'd been awaiting this very question. "Circles are the perfect shape. Every angle is the correct angle. And biscuits of this size—scarcely larger than a guinea—need not be cut or trimmed. They are already the ideal size to pop into one's mouth. Try it!"

He did not. "And the colorful dollops at the center of each?"

"Spring fruits. Only the very best," she added with a straight face. "Hand-selected by the sixth duke of—"

"There are five shades of pink or red, three

shades of purple... One cannot even tell which fruit is which."

"I should hope not," she said cheerfully. "The mystery is part of the magic. Your guests do not show their true identities. Why then should their biscuits?"

"Because they're *biscuits*," he growled.

It was a clever idea. He could already see the appeal of each guest filling a small plate with half a dozen shortbread guineas and exclaiming in delight to discover this one was that flavor, and so on.

"You're *pretending* to hate the idea," she scolded him.

He glowered at her.

"Before you say it's not pretentious enough for your set because they'll only eat buttered *tellines* simmered by a Parisian chef—"

"Aix-en-Provence," Julian murmured.

"—allow me to counter by pointing out that an exalted Aix-en-Provence-ian chef should be capable of duplicating this recipe, and that the very conceit of biscuits with secret identities is by definition pretentious. Pretentious and delicious. Try one," she coaxed. "Unmask its flavor."

He lifted one that looked like blackberry and placed in his mouth.

It was not blackberry. It was elderberry. The surprise was indeed as satisfying as Miss Thorne had promised.

The biscuit itself was of the ideal diameter to pop into one's mouth with ease and grace. The creamy dollop of tartness on top was the perfect balance to the sweet, crumbly shortbread. It was a superlative biscuit.

"How does it taste?" Miss Thorne asked eagerly.

"Insufficiently pretentious," he informed her. "Un-French. I think these were made with asymmetrical elderberries."

She clapped her hands. "You love it! I knew you would! Your guests would too, if you let them."

This did not require a reply. She already knew he would reject all changes. He helped himself to what looked like a gooseberry biscuit.

It was strawberry-rhubarb.

Miss Thorne leaned forward. "Perhaps no one has ever told you, so allow me to be the first. Relinquishing a minute fraction of control does not diminish your power nor compromise your self. It is still your house and it remains your masquerade, regardless of the menu one finds at the refreshment table."

"And it is my reputation at risk," he added.

She rolled her eyes. "Ah, yes, your reputation for debauchery and complete disregard of polite society's rules. Are your guests really going to be offended if individual biscuit flavors are unlabeled and the shortbread does not come from France?"

"Deeply offended," he told her. "*Mortally* offended. I shall be at the top of all of the scandal columns by morning."

"You... what?" Miss Thorne's eyes widened, and her mouth fell open. "*Tomorrow* morning?"

"You did not expect me to eat four dozen bite-sized biscuits by myself, did you?" He was not giving in just to please her. He was proving her wrong. He was still in control.

"I..." She blinked at him.

"We'll put them on the tray nearest the dance floor. That is the most frequented of all the dessert tables. There aren't enough to last for more than a quarter hour, but that should be enough time to gauge the general reaction. If I hear so much as a whisper of complaint against these shortbread guineas—"

"You won't," she promised. "Anyone who dislikes 'masquerade biscuits' shall be deposited in the Thames before they can ruin the experience for other guests."

"You're ruthless," he said. "I like it."

She brightened. "You do?"

"Haven't you fathomed out by now that it is *you* I like?" He gave into temptation and pulled her into his arms.

*J*ulian did not give Miss Thorne's bewitching lips time to formulate an impertinent response.

He kissed her instead.

Her mouth tasted like fresh fruit. Tart and sweet. A combination he was coming to associate with her and her kisses.

Julian hated not being in control, yet that was exactly how he felt whenever he was near Miss Thorne. It wasn't the biscuits that concerned him. It was the odd sensation of being drawn to her *because* she forced him to unbend, despite his express wishes.

Even now, with her inviting warmth and soft curves pressed against him, he could not state with certainty that this embrace had transpired because he'd hauled her to him like a boor of low breeding.

He suspected Miss Thorne had known from the moment she entered the green parlor whether any kissing would be taking place within its walls today.

In any case, he was glad for it. He had hungered for her mouth, for her arms about his neck, for her breasts pressed against him, ever since she'd stepped out of his carriage after the market and disappeared.

No—ever since he'd first tasted her lips on the steps of his ballroom.

That he had got his wish, and his hands could now trace the curve of her spine, and the swell of her hips, did not dampen his ardor in the least. He wanted more. He hungered not just for her kisses, but for the feel of every curve rubbing delectably against the hardness of his body.

She was all edges when they argued—sharp tongue, sharp mind—but when she was in his arms, everything about her was pleasingly soft. He loved the softness of her hair, the softness of her skin, the plump softness filling out her gown to perfection.

He wanted to rend her gown from her frame and feast upon all that softness with his mouth. Caress her, tease her, tempt her, until her passion burned just as bright as his own. Then he'd sink his hard shaft beneath her thighs and—

Julian tore his lips from hers before he could act on his thoughts. His heart beat erratically. Guests would be arriving within the hour. He must be in the ballroom to greet them.

"These kisses mean nothing," he reminded her.

And reminded himself.

Life had proven time and again that Julian could keep the *things* he held dear, but not the people.

It was good that he'd long ago hardened his heart. Kissing was just physical. Something he did for a moment's enjoyment, like eating a shortbread guinea with a dollop of blueberry. Delicious while it lasted, and then easily forgotten.

"I remember your rules." Miss Thorne did not look chastened. "If *you* have trouble remembering, you should write them down in your spontaneity diary."

"In my... what?"

She rose from his lap and picked up a large canvas bag from beside the sofa.

His focus had been so consumed with kissing her, he hadn't even registered the bag's presence.

She loosened the drawstrings, reached inside, and handed him a small brown book.

"What is this?" he asked suspiciously.

"I just told you," she said. "Spontaneity diary. My, you *do* need to write things down."

She held out a pencil.

He ignored it.

Instead, he opened the book. It was mostly unmarked, save for the headers labeled prettily at the top of each page.

The first sheet read, "17 April, 1819."
Beneath that:

Planned Spontaneity:
None

Achieved Spontaneity:
Biscuits
Kissing
Costume

"There's no such thing as *planned* spontaneity," he informed her.

"Not for normal people," she agreed.

He turned the page. Every day was a different date. Most were blank. Only Saturdays held the labels "Planned Spontaneity" and "Achieved Spontaneity."

"You expect me to... schedule moments in which I deviate from my own rules?"

"Baby steps," she told him. "One per week. It's like exercising an atrophied limb. You won't cease being an uptight, rigid sobersides overnight, but with time and practice, perhaps you'll become marginally more tolerable."

He cut her a quelling gaze. "Flattering."

She fluttered her eyelashes at him. "Look

how much you've accomplished, just in one day!"

He re-read the prefilled list. "What do you mean by 'costume'? I never wear—"

"Ah-ah-ah." She shook her finger. "An uptight, rigid sobersides might have such limitations, but a spontaneous soul such as yours would never say 'never.'"

She pulled a mask out of her bag.

He stared at it. "What is that?"

"A mask," she said helpfully. "It goes on your face."

"I don't want it."

She pulled out another just like it. "Mine matches yours. Isn't that adorable?"

"Why would I wish to seem adorable?"

"You wouldn't," she said. "That's the entire point. *No one* will think it is you behind this mask. We can attend tonight's masquerade as an anonymous Lord and Lady X."

"Attend my own party," he repeated. "Anonymously."

"Just think of it," she coaxed. "You can stand next to the refreshment table and administer a forty-question quiz to each guest who selects a shortbread, and no one will ever know the obnoxious Lord X was actually you!"

"It may have advantages," he admitted.

"One hour," she said. "If you hate it, you need only whip off the mask and shake the white powder from your hair—"

"Powder my *hair?*" Julian covered his brown locks protectively with his hands. "It would look gray!"

"It's a costume," Miss Thorne enunciated. "Are you really that vain?"

"Yes," he answered without hesitation. "Extremely vain and deservedly so."

"Good." She smiled at him. "Then it's an excellent costume."

Which was how Julian Newcombe-Ives, the sixth Duke of Lambley, found himself being cheered by a raucous group of joyful revelers as he and Miss Thorne stepped over the threshold arm in arm.

"Lord X! Lady X!"

Flutes of champagne flashed skyward all throughout the ballroom as the crowd roared with enthusiasm. A pair of footmen appeared at their sides with brimming trays of champagne-filled glasses, so that Lord and Lady X could take part in the fun.

And it *was* fun, Julian admitted grudgingly. Fun and awkward and interesting and uncomfortable and eye-opening.

Even with an ugly mask and powdered hair, he attracted plenty of admiring gazes—but no one fawned over him specifically or toasted his name.

Julian could not help but wonder how much of his popularity was *his* popularity at all. Were they here for him? Or because of his title? Or did they come simply because he threw one hell of a good party?

"Well, Lord X?" Miss Thorne opened her reticule to reveal a small notebook and pencil nub inside. "Shall we begin the 'masquerade biscuit' inquisition? Or shall we dance?"

"I do not dance," he reminded her.

"Our important host is too busy to dance," she corrected him. "Too busy controlling every tiny detail, no matter how insignificant. You, however, are the carefree and spontaneous Lord X."

He stared at her. Lord knew he'd like to have her in his arms again.

"I *do* have 'planned spontaneity' in my diary entry for today," he admitted.

She grinned at him, and he pulled her onto the parquet.

"Has anyone ever mentioned you are appallingly bossy and presumptuous?"

"You do." Her eyes twinkled. "Every time you see me."

"It is a repugnant quality," he informed her.

Or at least it should be. Instead of repelling him, each encounter only served to make him desire even more of her. What he wouldn't give for a wife like this! As a man accustomed to getting his way, being thwarted by fate rankled.

If only Miss Thorne had been born to the world of the ton...

Julian nearly stumbled at the direction of his

thoughts. He put that nonsense out of his mind at once. She *wasn't* beau monde. He was. *She* knew she would never be his duchess.

Yet she made him want things they both knew he could not have.

CHAPTER 13

Unity picked her way carefully down the slick cobblestone street. The rain had drizzled to a stop an hour ago, leaving uneven puddles and rivulets of dirty water in its wake.

Her mind was not on the spring weather. Nor were her constantly churning thoughts centered on the nest egg she was working to amass or the masquerade-themed assembly rooms she intended to one day own on a street just like this one.

She was thinking about the Duke of Lambley.

Again.

Still.

He had pushed the usual topics so far from her mind that thoughts of him had *become* the new usual.

Ridiculous. Pointless. They had spent a glorious hour dancing and arguing and laughing together as Lord and Lady X, but he was no carefree anonymous buck.

At precisely eleven o'clock, he had handed her his mask, knocked the powder from his hair, and resumed his role as king of the ballroom.

That had been Unity's cue to forget about her temporary employer.

Take advantage of being left to her own devices, inspect every carefully planned element, and then log in her book each stratagem and rationale and, hell, even the dimensions and angles of the triangle sandwiches.

And she *did*. She *had*. In between remembering his expressive lips crushed to hers and the feel of his strong arms cradling her close.

It wasn't even about the swan's teasing recommendation to accept the invitation to go upstairs with the duke if he asked. Unity didn't bother lying to herself about what she would do the next time. Of course she would go with him. She would drag him up the stairs by his cravat if it got them to a bedchamber faster.

That was the easy part. A meaningless tumble was something anyone could walk away from.

The hard part was making it meaningless.

She *liked* Lambley, damn him. She hadn't meant to or expected to. He was rich and white and powerful, born to a title and luxury and privilege. She'd expected stilted conversations at best, if he condescended to speak with her at all.

And they'd somehow become friends. More

than friends and less than friends, at the same time. He desired her enough to kiss her senseless, respected her enough to listen to her ideas... and yet, she only fit into his life one day a week, the twilight hour before the masquerade.

A temporary diversion. She couldn't let herself forget.

Ah, here she was. She hauled open the door to noisy, smoky Eshu's Altar and stepped inside.

"Miss Unity!" called out dozens of gamblers at once, some in obvious delight and others pretending to hide their cards or their chips from her view.

Normally she greeted them all by name with a smile or a teasing remark, but today she was struck at the parallels between Sampson's Cheapside gaming hell and Lambley's Mayfair masquerades.

Both locales greeted her with enthusiasm when she walked in the door. At the duke's, she was Lady X, one more anonymous face among many. Here, she was Miss Unity Thorne, appreciated for exactly who and what she was.

At Lambley's, liveried footmen surrounded her at once with silver trays piled artfully with crystal goblets of the finest champagne. Here, Sampson beckoned from the other side of the bar, one hand holding a glass of her favorite brandy and the other wiping down the counter with a worn brown rag.

Two wholly separate spheres, Unity reminded herself. This was the one she belonged to.

Sampson slid the glass of brandy across the counter toward Unity. "Heading to the theatre tonight?"

"Just came from there." She'd traded in the gown she'd just worn to Lambley's for a new one he hadn't yet seen.

"How are the actress friends?" He wiggled his brows. "I'm still waiting for you to introduce me."

"Anyone with half a brain should love to meet you, but you know how it is. They barely leave the theatre for long enough to go home and sleep. When you're not the star, you have to do whatever you can to stay employed."

That, and they were seeking protectors with money to burn.

"Now you have two posts." Sampson wiped the bar, but his eyes were on her. "Do *you* ever get to sleep?"

"Three posts." Unity held up her reticule and clinked the coins inside. "I intend to turn your clients' pockets inside out at the whist table today."

"Gambling is not employment," he chided her.

She sipped her brandy. "Rich, coming from a man who has built his fortune on that exact enterprise."

"I manage the venue," he reminded her. "I

don't sit at the tables. Have you ever considered slowing down?"

"Slowing... down?" She stared at him, appalled.

"You run headlong into things. Into everything."

"If I see something I can do, I do it," she said defensively.

"Here are a few things you could do." He ticked them off on his fingers. "Slow down. Breathe. Have a moment when you're not running yourself ragged."

"I have to work harder than everyone else if I'm to have a chance at succeeding," she said. "People tell me my dreams are impossible. I'm a woman. I'm Black. I've no one I can count on but myself. But I know I can become a successful business owner if I try hard enough. *You* did it."

"I'm not a woman," Sampson said dryly. "And I didn't do it on my own. You helped me, just like you helped your cousin. Perhaps you could make a living out of helping others build their businesses."

Help privileged men get richer and more powerful? She shook her head. There was enough of that already. "I want to fulfill my potential, not someone else's. I'm tired of being employed. I want to be the manager, not the managed."

Sampson inclined his head. He might not

know the intricacies of being a woman, but he intimately knew the difficulties of being Black. Whilst slavery had technically always been illegal on England's shores, Britain had yet to abolish the horrid practice throughout its territories. They both had family members they would never see again, cousins and ancestors they would never know at all.

If being free meant owning a gaming hell for Sampson, he would accept without question whatever Unity needed, in order to feel like her own person. To be in charge of herself, subject to nobody's whims but her own.

A cry rose from a Hazard table. After an exchange of coins, the gentlemen put down their dice and came up to the bar for fresh ales.

Sampson poured with practiced efficiency and slid the frothy ales across the counter to the men. "Downing, Bost, Grenville."

Unity placed her brandy glass on the bar. "I'm for the whist table."

"Wait." Sampson motioned her toward the storage pantry they'd often used to have a quick word in privacy.

As soon as they were out of earshot from the men at the bar, Unity raised her brows. "Are you going to lecture me?"

"I don't want to lecture," Sampson said softly, his dark brown eyes unsettlingly astute. "I want to help. You don't have to wear your feet to the bone chasing after dreams, Unity."

She scoffed. "I should repose on a chaise longue and allow the dreams to come to me?"

"It's an option." His eyes clouded, then cleared. "Marry me. I already have a successful business. We've managed it together before. We can do it again. I'll buy you that chaise longue, and you can 'repose' whenever you like."

Not again. Unity looked away.

Sampson was a good man. A great friend. He would make a wonderful husband... to someone else.

She liked him too much to saddle him with a bride who didn't love him, not in that way. A wife who would resent him for convincing her to give up her dreams in order to help him build his.

"I thank you for your kind offer," she said quietly. "It is not what I am looking for at this time."

He tilted his head. "What *are* you looking for?"

Autonomy, freedom, financial independence. Those had been her aims for so long, the words usually spilled from her tongue without any conscious thought.

She was startled to discover a new word had crept onto the list.

Love.

She wanted *love*. Her achievements would be lonely without someone to share them with. She wanted someone who challenged her and believed in her. Someone who didn't want to save her or fix her or do her a favor.

To Unity, Sampson's gaming hell would always remind her of the worst moments of her life. When she had nowhere else to go because her cousin had turned her out. She had been eaten alive by betrayal and fear and hatred. Meanwhile, her cousin Roger was actively trying to drive Sampson out of business, so she'd funneled all that rage into making this gaming hell outshine anything her cousin had ever touched.

It worked. They won. But this place would always be Sampson's. Unity's emotions about her time here were too raw and ugly to let her stay for long.

Sampson deserved to fall in love with someone who could fully appreciate him for the beautiful soul that he was.

"You know I'd be a dreadful wife to you."

His lips quirked. "I've made my peace with that."

"You shouldn't have to. One of the advantages to not being ton is that we get to choose. Don't settle for anything less than a love match, Sampson."

His brown eyes widened in obvious surprise. "I've never heard you talk about love. I didn't think it figured into your plans."

"I didn't either," she admitted. "Maybe I'm growing."

"Maybe you grew a long time ago and are

only just now letting go of who you used to be." He angled his head. "Or maybe you've already fallen in love with someone."

"I'm too busy for love at the moment." She patted the bag at her side. "I've got a thick journal brimming with the plans I'm making for my future assembly rooms, and I—"

"May I see them?" he asked with obvious interest.

Unity pulled the book from her bag and handed it to him with pride.

He flipped carefully through the pages.

"I think," he said at last, "your assembly rooms will be an instant success. I also cannot help but notice that a significant number of these entries are dedicated not to your future endeavors, but to the betterment of a certain weekly masquerade already in existence?"

She yanked the book from his hands. "I'm helping him."

"I've no doubt."

"It's business," she added firmly.

He nodded. "So you said."

"I'm not going to marry him," she said defensively.

"Probably not," Sampson agreed. "Though I suppose we do have Queen Charlotte, so there is some precedent."

"Is there?" Unity shook her head. "Her African heritage is distant and minimal, whilst mine is present and obvious. Her mother was a princess. Mine descended from East Indies slaves. Her father was a duke. Mine was a preacher's son. She was born into royalty. Have you *seen* my rented rooms? Our paths and our stations could not be more different."

"So you *have* thought about this," Sampson said. "Interesting."

Unity clamped her teeth shut.

"If anyone can do the impossible, it's you," he told her. "If that's the dream you've set your sights on, go after it."

"I don't think I'd want to be part of that world," she said uncertainly. "They would call me an unworthy social climber and much, much worse. If I were an heiress or shared blood with royalty, the color of my skin would be less of a deterrent. There would be looks and whispers and doors that did not open, but plenty of doors would. My unforgivable crime is being common and poor."

"I've never met anyone more uncommon," Sampson replied. "If your duke doesn't have cork for brains, he sees it, too."

She shook her head. "Even if he were interested, he couldn't choose me. He *is* the beau monde. Opening myself up for an inevitable rejection would be foolish."

And painful. Just the thought of being so vulnerable had her adding more protective layers around her heart.

"All Lambley and I share is a temporary business arrangement." And torrid, but equally temporary kisses. She would enjoy it while it lasted and then walk away with her head high. "I'll fall in love with someone appropriate to my station once I've achieved my other aims and have time for softer emotions."

"Mm-hm," Sampson said. "Then I wish you luck. You're going to need it."

On Saturday afternoon, Julian was not in his office managing his affairs or in the ballroom preparing for the upcoming masquerade.

He was seated at a long table in the front dining room whose tall, mullioned windows had the best vantage point of the front path.

Not that there was much to see at the moment. It had been alternately drizzly and foggy all morning, and a great cloud of white mist had settled over Grosvenor Square. The terraced homes of his neighbors were not visible in such conditions, but then again, Julian wasn't stealing glances out of the front window in the hopes of glimpsing a neighbor.

He was thinking about Miss Thorne. He was always thinking about Miss Thorne. She wouldn't arrive for hours. The mere fact that the sun had not yet set proved him ridiculously eager and early. Yet here he was, seated at an empty dinner table, pretending unsuccessfully to be concentrating on the correspondence before him.

Heath Grenville had sent another report.

Julian was dying to read it. The report was right there in his hands. Unopened. Waiting.

Because part of him regretted ever asking for it. He wanted to know everything there was to know about Miss Thorne, but not like this. It wasn't even the reason he'd asked Grenville to investigate in the first place.

At the time, Julian had just wished to be certain that the beautiful, confounding stranger did not have questionable motives. If he'd learned anything so far, it was that the person with questionable motives was Julian himself.

He had employed her without any intention of putting her to work or taking her advice, and subsequently embarked on a campaign of passionate embraces that likewise were not destined to go anywhere at all.

In either case, what did it matter if he did not possess her precise street address? He didn't plan on visiting. If she kept her private life secret and separate from him, who cared? He had no plans to become a part of her life, or to make her part of his.

Anything contained in the document beneath his fingertips was therefore superfluous and irrelevant.

He ripped open the seal anyway and devoured the text inside.

Miss Thorne, it seemed, frequented a gambling den called Eshu's Altar, situated in a working-class section of town, and catering to that audience. Most of the clients were men, many of whom numbered among London's twenty thousand Black citizens, and all of whom seemed to hold Miss Thorne in the utmost esteem.

Long-term customers greeted her by name. She seemed to enjoy a particularly personal connection with the owner, a Mr. Sampson Oakes, who not only kept a bottle of Miss Thorne's favorite brandy at the ready, but she was also not charged for any refreshments consumed, nor required to pay the table fee when gambling.

It was not recommended to bet against her at whist.

Julian slammed the report closed and shoved it away. There. Did he feel better now? Perhaps this Mr. Oakes was a past or current lover. Perhaps Eshu's Altar was Miss Thorne's hunting ground, and the reason he hadn't heard of her before was because she was a demimondaine who catered to a completely different neighborhood.

None of these things were in Julian's control or, more to the point, any of his business. Just because he had the money and the connections to uncover her secrets without her consent did not mean he ought to be doing so. He crumpled the report into a ball.

Even if Miss Thorne appeared on his doorstep bearing an annotated history of her entire life for Julian's perusal, what would it change?

From the moment she'd shown up uninvited with a calling card that read *Miss Thorne, Courtesan,* he'd known she was completely unsuitable. What's more, amorous attention from him wasn't even why she had come to his door.

Julian drew ink and paper toward him and quickly penned a response to Heath Grenville, thanking him for his attention to detail and informing him his services were no longer necessary.

Once this was dry and sealed with wax, Julian jotted another letter to his man of business, requesting Mr. Grenville to receive twice the agreed upon sum, in compensation for his efforts and to show that the abrupt dissolution of their agreement was not out of dissatisfaction with Grenville.

Julian was cross with himself.

He tossed the crumpled report into the fire, then rang the bell pull for a footman to deliver the pair of missives.

Now he should be able to concentrate on important matters.

He could not.

How much time remained before the masquerade? He swiveled to look. *Four hours?* He really ought to have someone service his clock. Clearly the minute hand was not progressing as quickly as it ought.

He'd told Miss Thorne to arrive an hour earlier than usual, which was somehow still three hours away, no matter how often he checked the time.

The rain started again. Fitting. Perhaps it would wash away this absurd obsession. That's what this was. The only thing it could be. Julian was incapable of other emotions. He hadn't used his heart in decades.

The fact that he could not get Miss Thorne out of his head, the galling way he counted down each second until he could see her again—it was a trick of the brain, nothing more. The allure of scarcity. Diamonds were expensive because they were rare. Young bucks angled for Almack's subscriptions because they were difficult to obtain.

The solution, therefore, was to spend *more* time with her, not less. Once his muddled brain realized she was an ordinary person like any other, once he saw that every encounter was merely more of the same, the spell would be broken and he could move on.

Horses clopped outside the window. A hackney, in this neighborhood, in front of Julian's home?

He shot out of the dining room and down the corridor to the primary entryway before the butler could turn the handle on the front door.

"At ease, Barnaby." Julian plucked the umbrella from his butler's hand and strode out into the rain to accompany Miss Thorne up the path.

"Why, Mr. Barnaby," she said, her brown eyes

twinkling. "You look unusually dapper today. Did you do something different with your hair?"

"It's me," Julian whispered. "Don't tell anyone."

He centered the umbrella over her bonnet to give her the most protection from the drizzle. This meant one of Julian's coat sleeves was getting damp, but a coat could be exchanged for another.

He led her into the house. "I told you to arrive precisely one hour prior to the masquerade."

She widened her eyes. "I assumed you meant *four* hours."

"I meant eight," he growled. "You're late."

He pulled her into the first open parlor, closed the door behind them, and claimed her mouth in a kiss.

The umbrella fell to the floor.

His hands were about her waist. Her fingers twined in his hair. They banged against the wainscoting, their bodies pressed together, Miss Thorne's spine against the wall, and Julian's chest and hips and thighs flush against her softness.

Her mouth was as hungry as his, her hands just as seeking. He had thought he had the position of power in pinning her against the wall, but in doing so he had blocked off access to half of her body. His was the one exposed to her fingers gliding over his shoulders, his upper arms, his back. Despite the many layers covering his flesh, he felt her touch all the way to the hot skin beneath.

He did not want to share her. Could not. *Would* not.

"While... *this* is happening between us," he said between kisses, "your mouth is not to be engaged in this activity with anyone else. Understand? If this causes you a loss in income, tell me the number, and I will double it."

She pulled back from his kiss with a bemused expression. "The king of one-night trysts with masked strangers is asking for mutual monogamy?"

He glared at her.

"Oh, not *mutual*. Just me, whilst you carry on as usual." She wrinkled her nose. "I decline."

His tone hardened. "What did you say?"

"I said, no thank you." She lifted a shoulder. "Either we both kiss whomever we want, or we exclusively kiss each other."

The person he wanted *was* her. Both choices were the same thing.

"I'll triple your earnings," he said. "Quadruple."

"Use the money to clean out your ears," she suggested. "Either we're equal, or we're nothing."

"Fine," he ground out. "We are both bound by the same rules. No liaisons of any sort with anyone else, until I say we're done."

"Unless I say it first." She smiled up at him cheerfully. "Mutual monogamy it is, then."

"Stop saying that word!"

She opened her mouth—likely to argue with him—and he caught her lips with his own to silence her.

Yes, yes, it was mutual monogamy. An agreement he had never contemplated entering until such time as he'd chosen a wife. That he should do so with Miss Thorne...

It meant nothing. He was a meticulous tactician, and this was the most efficient way to achieve his aim of being the only man in Miss Thorne's life... For now.

Once he found the perfect bride, he would have to let her go.

CHAPTER 15

Unity didn't just kiss him back. She gripped the hard muscle of the Duke of Lambley's upper arms and held on tight. He kissed her as though he were a long-lost sailor, reuniting with his true love again after endless years at sea.

Instead, Unity was the drowned rat.

Wind had turned her umbrella inside-out days ago, and she hadn't had time to shop for a new one. The rain had tripled her hair's already impressive natural volume, and turned the jaunty feathers of her bonnet into limp, wet bits of confetti littering her black curls.

The section of gown sticking out from beneath her pelisse was drenched with equal parts drizzle and puddle.

And Lambley—seemed not to notice any of it. He looked at her as though she were the leading lady, starring in the most celebrated opera of the century. He touched her as though she were beautiful, not bedraggled.

As for him... Had there ever been a man more fine?

She'd taken him by surprise. The masquerade wasn't for hours. Yet he was groomed as though the Queen herself might stop by at any moment to have a cup of tea. His coat fit him to perfection. His cravat was a work of art. And his soft brown hair... was rakishly rumpled, thanks to Unity's fingers sliding through it to bring his lips closer to hers.

When at last he released her from his arms, there was nowhere else she wished to be. But the expression on his handsome face was so mischievous, she was immediately on her guard.

"What is it?" she asked suspiciously.

"It's... spontaneity day!" He grinned at her.

She blinked at him. "What?"

He crossed the parlor in two strides and lifted a familiar-looking book from a side table.

It was the diary she'd brought him. With the schedule she'd teased could help him unbend a tiny bit.

He was *using* it.

Maybe.

She crossed her arms. "Why is your spontaneity calendar still right here in this parlor? Did you leave it behind and forget all about it?"

"I never leave anything to chance."

"You pulled me into a random room," she pointed out.

He smiled. "It was designed to look that way."

The duke opened his journal and pointed at today's entry, which read:

Miss Thorne will spontaneously arrive early.
Be ready with the grapes.

"IT'S NOT VERY spontaneous of me if it's easily anticipated," she grumbled, then read the list again. "'Grapes?'"

Lambley gestured toward a long sideboard upon which a golden silk cloth covered a trio of odd-shaped mounds. With a flourish, he whisked the cloth away to reveal three impeccably polished silver-topped platters resting on trays filled with chopped ice.

He really *had* brought her into a room he'd specifically prepared in anticipation of her early visit.

"What grapes?" she asked again.

He lifted the first delicate silver lid to reveal a sprig of half a dozen dark purple grapes the size of blueberries.

"What a... feast," she said faintly.

"I *have* surprised you." He grinned with satisfaction. "These grapes aren't properly meant to be consumed the way one might eat a normal grape, but we're being spontaneous."

"They're not normal grapes?"

"They're the best seasonal grapes from my three favorite vintners. I have searched all over for the best wines to serve at my gatherings and these vineyards produce the best of the best." He lifted the other lids.

She gazed at equally small bunches of equally small grapes.

He lifted one. "It took a bit of finesse to procure these choice specimens, but no challenge is too daunting for spontaneity day. Today we shall enjoy artisan-crafted wine from Florence, Spain, and France, and sample the very grapes each varietal comes from."

Of course he would casually unveil an assortment of grapes from his favorite wineries, which had shipped sprigs of fresh fruits to him from three different countries, just so Lambley could surprise Unity on Planned Spontaneity Day.

It was extravagant and foolish and adorable.

"All right," she said. "Tell me about your grapes and your wines."

He uncovered a fourth platter farther down the sideboard to reveal a dish piled high with nuts, seeds, and bite-sized cheeses of all varieties. Quickly, he arranged a sampling—"to adjust the palate"—and placed it on a small round table between two armchairs.

Next, he arranged not two, but six crystal goblets. He uncorked three different bottles and poured an inch of wine into each of the glasses.

"Don't worry," he assured her. "Whichever wines you like best, you can have more of."

"I wasn't worried," she managed.

Lambley was many things, but stingy was not one of them.

In short order, he was seated beside her, explaining what kind of soil was best for each grape, and warning her that the skins were thicker, and the interiors riddled with seeds, but the flesh would be sweeter than the sort of grapes she was used to.

She placed one in her mouth carefully and bit down. The grape exploded with sweetness, tempered by the bitterness of its crunchy seeds and its oddly chewy skin.

"What do you think?" he asked.

She wrinkled her nose. "I don't know yet."

He laughed. "They're not meant to be eaten, really. They're meant to be drunk. See if you like this better."

Lambley handed her a goblet.

She swirled the wine and tried to admire its movement knowingly, as though she had any idea what anyone divined from the liquid streaks forming on their glasses.

"I have no idea what I'm looking at," she said at last.

While he explained, she ate a few nuts and a piece of cheese, then clinked her glass with his and brought the wine to her lips.

It was delicious. Abominably delicious.

She had absolutely no doubt he had taken it

upon himself to sample every wine on the Continent, because surely there could not be one better than this. It was oaky and fruity, dry and smooth.

"Well?" he prompted.

"It's the best wine I've ever tasted," she admitted.

His boyish grin lit the room. "Just wait until you try the others, Miss Thorne."

"I think you've earned the right to call me Unity," she said with a laugh. "If I drink all this wine, I'll be singing sea-songs without the least hint of proper comportment."

"Unity," he repeated softly, then leaned back, his eyes hooded as he considered her.

Her cheeks burned. "Don't worry, you needn't share your—"

"Julian," he answered. "To be used only in private. I cannot allow others to suspect I'm a human with a Christian name."

He was teasing her. The Duke of Lambley—er, Julian—was well aware of his haughty reputation, but of course he must also have friends.

And was treating her like one of them.

"Now," he said. "This next grape..."

She questioned him on every detail, doing her best to commit every nuance about this evening to memory. The sweetness of the grapes, the savory nuts and cheeses, the crunchy bitterness of the seeds.

But most of all, she wanted to remember

how this moment felt. The Duke of Lambley, patient and teasing, charmingly delighted every time a grape or a wine pleased her.

It almost felt as though... he were wooing her.

Which could not be.

She was temporary. He had been clear. *She* had been clear. He was in the market for a very specific bride, and if this interlude proved anything, it was that Unity could not be less suited for the role. There was no sense pretending otherwise.

He was a duke. A baroness would be beneath him. The thought of wedding a textiles heiress, laughable. Unity was not even that lofty. She was neither titled nor rich nor a pale English rose or any of the other requirements on his list.

A list he no doubt possessed.

Any man as exacting as Julian, a duke who accepted nothing less than the absolute best in everything he touched, ate, acquired, or otherwise, likely possessed a list of bridal requirements so precise, only one woman in all the world could possibly fill the role.

And it wasn't Unity.

Courting her would be more scandalous than hosting his lavish weekly bacchanalia. Invitations would cease, out of fear he'd bring his low-born Black wife along. Memberships, dropped. His life, irrevocably curtailed.

Not just his. He'd said his primary concern

was to provide the best path for his privileged, proper heirs, who would be welcomed by the ton and find happiness amongst their peers. A noble, understandable, worthy desire for one's children.

And something Unity could not offer.

She set down her wine. That was enough pretending to be courted. She was not here for him. Unity was here to learn all she could about hosting successful, popular masquerades that kept people coming back for more. She should worry about her future, not Lambley's.

"How did you advertise your parties?" she asked. "I cannot imagine you sending an invitation to every name in the peerage."

His lips twitched. "Hardly. My little soirées started on a much smaller scale than what you see now. I had to know the person would not only covet the opportunity but also follow the rules before I sent an invitation."

Of course he would have rules. And assess each person individually to determine their suitability.

"What if I had a friend I'd like to bring to the party?" she asked.

"Do you?" He arched a brow. "Bring her. Or him."

Her mouth fell open. "*You* would let *me* invite some stranger, sight unseen? Your Grace, the Duke of Controlling Every Detail?"

"Either I trust your judgment, or I don't," he replied. "I do. Why else would I be experimenting with the lists of ideas you force upon me?"

She stared at him. "You're taking my advice?"

"Only a fool believes himself the only one capable of good judgment. My balls are as crowded as they are, because every friend I extend a personal invitation to *also* has friends. And those friends have friends, and so on. Everyone knows their invitation hinges on respecting other guests' anonymity and autonomy."

She nodded. "No pressuring anyone to do anything they don't wish, from going upstairs to dancing a minuet. And no sharing names."

He inclined his head. "If the friend of a friend should prove untrustworthy, then so is the person who recommended them, both of whom are immediately removed from the premises."

"Permanent expulsion, all the way down the line." She pantomimed a shudder. "With that threat hanging over them, I doubt many would risk recommending someone whose character they weren't absolutely sure of."

"I've only had to remove a guest once." Julian's expression hardened. "He was in his cups, but intoxication is not an acceptable excuse."

"I'm guessing there's *no* acceptable reason to break one of your rules?"

"There is no excuse for not being in complete control of one's self," he replied, his eyes and tone gone dark.

She tried to lighten the mood. "Certainly children—"

"—are not exempt," he snapped. "Nor am I."

She swallowed. Whatever this was, it was personal. "Did something happen?"

CHAPTER 16

For a brief second, the anger vanished from the duke's eyes, replaced by an anguished look of such deep sorrow, Unity immediately regretted having pried.

"I'm sorry," she said quickly. "You don't have to tell me."

He turned from her and poured a glass of wine, then set down the bottle without taking his goblet. Instead, he sank back in his seat and lifted a pocket watch from his coat.

"My father gave this to me. I haven't wound it in years. The hands are frozen at six o'clock." Julian's voice was gravelly. "He was angry at me for misbehaving. The last thing he ever said to me was, 'We'll be home at six. Have yourself under control by then.'"

Her throat tightened in horror. "How old were you?"

"Eight." He cleared his throat. "My uncle was my last remaining family member and my interim guardian. I could not act as duke until I reached my majority."

"What happened?"

"Uncle took over my childhood home and began making changes. Rearranging rooms my mother had decorated. Claiming my father's bedchamber and study as his own. Acting like a king, even though he was not. Ordering me about as though I were a pageboy, and not the Duke of Lambley."

"Oh," she whispered. *Oh.*

No wonder he could not withstand the feeling of not being in control of his environment. He would forever associate powerlessness with the grief of loss and all the hurtful changes it had wrought. His need for control had also saved his life. Perhaps to Julian, it still did. And to let go of that control would feel like diving into the sea without knowing how to swim.

"I outranked my self-important uncle, but was underage and unable to stand in his way. Despite an out-of-control affinity for gin, Uncle had my 'best interests' at heart. He sent me away from the small comfort of my family home and off to school."

Unity nodded. Another abrupt, unwanted change.

Julian smiled grimly. "The old spotted fool died from too much drink. Mere months before I was to gain my majority. Chaos erupted. There was no other family member to serve as guardian, no man to take the reins of the estate."

"And then it was your turn," she said softly.

He'd gone from powerless to all-powerful overnight, without the benefit of years of tutelage at his father's elbow. He would have been forced to learn on his own and quickly. By experimenting, by refining, by foregoing sleep until he reached the impossible aim of perfection.

Julian looked down at the watch in his hand. "If I had listened to my father... If I had been able to control myself, back then..."

"What could you have done if you had gone with them?" she asked. "You were a child, not a god. You could not have saved them. The accident would have claimed one more victim."

"We would have left earlier," he said. "If we'd set out on time as planned, we would have crossed the bridge *before* it fell. My lack of self-control..."

"Did *not* kill your family," she said firmly, sick at the heavy guilt a helpless child had been carrying since that awful day. "It was an accident, Julian. A terrible one, a horrible one. But an accident. Accidents can happen to anyone."

"Not to me." He drew himself tall. "Not if you plan properly and control everything around you. I haven't lost a loved one since."

Because he didn't *have* any.

Her heart wrenched. Julian had lost everyone he cared about, everyone he was close to, in one ghastly moment. Since that day, he surrounded himself with people, without ever allowing any of them close. He was the ton Bacchus, patron saint of anonymous encounters with strangers. And what he longed for most were real connections.

The one thing he could not allow himself to have.

No wonder he never repeated his liaisons. He would not risk his heart becoming involved. Julian already knew what the pain of losing someone he loved was like. He could not control accidents, but he could wall himself up and never love again.

"I was seven when I was orphaned," she said softly. "Old enough to remember what it was like to have a family. To be loved."

His hazel eyes met hers.

"And then I became the ward of my cousin." Her mouth tasted sour. "He didn't want me. He had a better chance of moving up without me hanging on, weighing him down."

Julian's lips tightened, but he did not interrupt.

"I had thought my family extremely well off," she said with a humorless laugh. "I didn't know what extravagance was until the day I moved in with Roger. He spared no expense—on himself. I was a fly to be swatted away."

"But you were family."

"He wished it were not so. Roger Thorne is white and a man, both of which characteristics gave him a significant advantage over me, and the maternal half of my family. Though he and I are paternal first cousins, Roger was not my friend."

Julian inclined his head. He was white and a man and a duke, but he'd had a taste of the dangers power imbalances could cause.

"Roger does not have friends," she continued, "because Roger is insufferable. Which was a big part of the reason the fashionable gentlemen's club he built sat unvisited for years, costing more to maintain than it raised in dues."

"I've heard of his club."

She smiled. "I'm not surprised. When it first opened, I was my cousin's ward. It would have been scandalously improper for a young lady to attend a gentlemen's club as a guest, but Roger saw no ethical argument against dressing his adolescent cousin as a maid and saving a few pence on servants' wages."

Julian grimaced. "He didn't pay you?"

"A pittance. He felt I should be grateful for room and board." Her lips twisted. "I was an excellent maid. The other staff said I had the skills to become a housekeeper at a grand estate and earn more money in a month than the entire lot of us did all year working for Roger."

"Did you try to find a post in a better house?"

She shook her head. "The thought of being 'rich'—which is what a housekeeper's two hundred guinea per annum sounded like to a fifteen-year-old girl—was attractive, indeed. But I didn't want to take orders from someone else.

My mind moved too quickly, and I had ideas of my own."

"What you didn't have was an opportunity to use them."

"Until I did. It all started when my cousin's man of business walked out after one of Roger's fits, never to return. Roger hadn't the least idea what his man of business *did* or how to decipher the journals of accounts."

"But you did?"

"I did. Being a maid didn't take *all* day—not anymore. My first act had been to restructure and re-delegate tasks so that everyone on staff had more time. Roger didn't know the difference. I enjoyed frequent conversations with the other employees, most of whose posts I briskly rearranged into easier, more efficient versions of the drudgery they'd once held."

"I imagine they loved you for it."

"We were a family of sorts," she said. "And my gamble worked. When Roger realized I could fill the role of man of business, what purpose was there in scrounging up some other feckless employee to pay, when his cousin could do the task for pennies?"

"No raise in wages?"

"Not a farthing. By then, I was eighteen and long out of the schoolroom. It was Roger who had arranged for my few tutors. By his count, I had a debt to pay, and taking this post would do nicely."

"You didn't send him to the devil?"

"I was in heaven," she admitted. "I was in *charge* of something for the first time in my life. My first decision was to make all of the decisions. I brought no correspondence to Roger unless absolutely necessary."

Which had suited him just fine, as it gave him more time to sip his fine brandy and brood sulkily out of the front window.

"Roger said it was unfair that his club was overlooked and ignored. Why, some no-account nobody had opened an embarrassingly gauche gaming hall in unfashionable Cheapside, and it already had more customers than Roger's fancy establishment."

Julian raised his brows in question.

"Eshu's Altar. I didn't know it then, but its owner, Sampson Oakes, would later become one of the best friends I ever had."

She took a sip from her wine as the memories washed over her.

"Roger hated him," she continued softly. "I was never certain if Sampson's greatest crime was being born poor or Black, or simply luckier than Roger. His humble gaming hell wasn't taking London by storm, but Sampson was doing better than Roger, which simply could not be borne. It was a travesty. A mockery. A personal attack on Roger's obvious superiority."

Unity rolled her eyes in disgust. She had learned to close her ears to her cousin's endless rants against the good fortune of a mortal enemy who didn't even know Roger's name.

"I presume Sampson's day-old cravat is cleverer than your cousin?"

Unity grinned. "You would win that wager. It was I who began the renovations on my cousin's club. Oh, how infuriated he had been, then! What was this? What were they doing? Who had authorized these changes?"

"His 'man' of business." Julian's lips curved. "And he couldn't gainsay you without looking incompetent himself."

"Not publicly," she agreed. "Then came the advertisements, posted without his permission or counsel. I barely ducked the bottle flying at my head for that. Roger might have throttled me with his bare hands, had a fashionable gentleman not chosen that moment to stride through the door and inquire about membership."

Julian leaned forward. "How did you do it?"

"I had let it be known that Roger's club was very, very exclusive. So exclusive, it was absolutely not open to new blood unless you had a current member who could vouch for you."

The duke frowned. "But I thought..."

"You're right. There *were* no current members. Which meant no one in the ton had anyone to vouch for them. Not that they would admit this failing to their peers. Instead, they showed up privately to plead their case, happy to pay thrice the annual subscription if Roger would please say, 'Oh, of course, Lord So-and-so has *always* been a member,' if anyone asked."

Julian burst out laughing. "Well played, man of business."

She made a little bow. "Once there were honest-to-god members, the nobs wasted no time in lording their status over their peers and doling out nominations and recommendations."

Roger's club would never be as crowded as White's or Brooks's, but every self-respecting gentleman would have a *membership* there, whether he made use of it or not. With the beau monde, appearances were everything.

The gamble worked. But Roger no longer needed her.

"When I dared to ask my cousin for a commission, he put me out into the street."

Julian looked appalled.

"I had no other family. The benevolent grandfather who had once helped those who had needed it most was long gone…as was the family fortune. No one could help me."

"What did you do?"

"I sought—and achieved—revenge by aiding Roger's rival: Sampson Oakes of Eshu's Altar. But that success wasn't enough. The gaming hell belonged to Sampson, just as the gentlemen's club belonged to Roger."

"I can only imagine how hollow that felt."

She nodded. "I decided I would make it on my own, on my terms. Prove myself. Follow *my* dreams, rather than build someone else's. But how? The only post I could manage was at the theatre, applying cosmetics."

"The beauty spot," he blurted out. "You had one, and then you didn't."

"Of course you would notice. Because you…" She stopped, throat thick, as she realized the reason. "Because you *saw* me. You looked at me, listened to me. Gave me a chance." She bit her lip, then pushed ahead. "It *is* all right to rely on others again, Julian. To have people you love and friends you worry about. It doesn't make you less."

"Not anymore." He rose from his chair without looking at her. "Guests will be arriving soon. I must prepare for the ball."

"Oh." She scrambled to her feet. "Of course. I'll just—"

Julian took a step toward the door, then turned around and pulled her into his embrace. He kissed her as though he drew renewed life from her lips, her tongue, her taste. He kissed her until she was breathless and trembling, until his own breath was ragged and his hands rough and demanding. Then he jerked back and stalked away without a word.

He didn't speak to her again for the rest of the night.

CHAPTER 17

*J*ulian leapt from his carriage in front of The Cloven Hoof, a gaming hell perched at the very edge of re-spectability.

That was how Julian felt, too. Teetering on the edge, his final fall determined by the direction of the wind.

He should not have investigated Miss Thorne. *Unity*. He should not have investigated Unity. Or first-named her. What the devil had he been thinking?

She was the upstanding one of the two. If he had just waited, she would have told him the things he'd paid a third party to find out. Once she trusted him enough to share.

Which she would have, if left to her own devices. Unity made close connections every time she stepped out of her house. The staff at her cousin's club adored her, the owner of that gaming hell, the actresses at the theatre. She'd made friends with Julian's night butler from the first how-do-you-do.

It was not a skill Julian possessed, but a trait he very much admired. He could surround himself with scores of people, but Unity managed to *belong* wherever she went.

Julian wanted to deserve her trust. More than that, he wanted to deserve *her*. Which was precisely why he should not have invited her to use his first name. No one had called him that in years. Why start now? Knowing their friendship could go nowhere?

He nodded at the burly guard securing the entrance. "Vigo."

"Your Grace." Vigo opened the door to allow him in.

The interior was as Julian remembered. The tables busy, the bar crowded. He met the harried gaze of one of the serving girls, and began to thread his way through the pockets of whist and faro toward the considerably quieter dining parlor on the opposite side of the gambling salon.

He knew what he wanted. Julian *always* knew what he wanted.

It wasn't Unity.

He needed a highborn, unobjectionable wife. A marriage of convenience to someone who wouldn't wriggle under his defenses. A woman who would beget a pair of perfect heirs, who themselves would grow up to be well-respected, perfect lords, so wholly unobjectionable as to be untainted by the sins in their father's past. Mostly because their mother had been such a high-ranking paragon since birth, overshadowing Julian's peccadillos with her golden halo.

But first, he had to make it through this gaming den.

At last, he burst free from the dicing and wagering and groans of remorse, and strode into the calm of the dining area.

"Lambley!"

Only one cluster of gentlemen gathered about a table. Its inhabitants immediately made room for the new arrival and smiled in welcome.

Lord Wainwright, an earl renowned for his angelic countenance. Lord Hawkridge, a marquess who had married a boarding school instructor. Heath Grenville, discreet arranger for the ton's little foibles. And Maxwell Gideon, the owner of the semi-respectable Cloven Hoof.

"I'll summon your favorite sherry," Max said.

"No need." Julian took the armchair next to him. "Your servers saw me enter."

Hawkridge raised his brows. "Then why the foul mood?"

Wainwright grinned. "It's because of a woman."

"What woman?" Julian growled.

"The one we're not supposed to know about," Wainwright answered, unrepentant.

Julian sent Grenville a deadly glare.

Grenville lifted his palms. "Not only did I say

nothing, my friend—but by glowering in my direction, you've not only confirmed Wainwright's wild suppositions, but implicated me in the matter as well."

"This is supposed to be where I come to relax," Julian grumbled.

"Trust me," Max said wryly. "No one comes to a gaming hell to relax."

"Trust me," Hawkridge added. "Lambley has never relaxed in his life."

"So tell us." Wainwright fluttered his blond lashes. "Is it love?"

"No," Julian said flatly.

He planned, so that he could control things. He controlled them, because he did not like risk. Nothing was riskier than love. The probability of being hurt made the experience not worth doing.

"I bet ten quid it's love," Wainwright stage-whispered to Hawkridge.

"Just because *you* four..." Julian began, then glowered at his friends. "You're all recently married. It's clouding your judgment."

"We're in love with our wives," Max said with a shrug.

"I recommend it," Wainwright added helpfully. "Love makes things easier."

"Love has never made anything easier," Julian said flatly.

"He's got it bad," Hawkridge whispered to Grenville. "Step three is denial."

Julian glared at him. "What are steps one and two?"

Hawkridge counted them on his fingers. "Step one, meeting her. I'd wager another ten you suspected you were in trouble then. Step two, crossing the line. Step three, denial. Step four, parson's trap."

"Crossing what line?" asked Julian sourly.

"Everyone has a different line," Wainwright answered. "But we all know it when we've crossed."

"Rubbish," Julian said. If that were the case, he possessed *dozens* of "lines."

Never see the same woman twice.

Never allow anyone close.

Never reveal anything personal.

Never first-name a woman, for God's sake.

And never, ever, ever—

"You can practically *see* him retracing his steps," Wainwright whispered. "He knows exactly when he crossed the line."

Hawkridge nodded. "Denial."

Julian folded his arms over his chest. "Amusing. Tell me this, at least. Are your wives more docile and easily controlled now that you've married them?"

All four men burst into guffaws of laughter.

"Good lord," said Max. "He *is* in denial if he thinks he has any chance of 'controlling' his marriage."

"Especially if it's to a woman worthy of being his match," Wainwright added. "She must be twice as Lambley as Lambley! I can't wait to meet her."

"Twice as—" Julian sputtered. "What does that even mean?"

"And just wait until you sire heirs," Hawkridge added. "I can attest that children are even less predictable than wives."

"I assure you," Julian said coldly, "*my* children will be the very pinnacle of—"

His sherry arrived, giving him the perfect opportunity to turn the subject to beverages, rather than Julian's carefully guarded heart.

He had believed himself incapable of feeling emotions like love for so long, that at first he failed to recognize the warmth suffusing his chest as he toasted his incorrigible, unapologetic friends.

Very well, he *could* feel love, of the platonic kind. He was not a monster. He cared for his friends. But romantic love... now there was a folly he would not be committing.

"For the sake of argument," said Hawkridge. "This woman that you don't love and aren't considering marrying. Do you like her?"

Julian glared at him. Of course he *liked* Unity. He wouldn't be puppeteering wine-and-cheese picnics from the most prestigious fields in all of Europe if he didn't *like* her.

"Because that's a good start," Hawkridge continued. "Grenville here married someone with whom he would never have dreamed of aligning himself, all because he liked her and one thing led to another."

"Grenville's case is different than mine," Julian informed him curtly.

Wainwright leaned forward with interest. "Too wide of a social gap? Or not wide enough?"

Grenville had married the country-bred poor relation of a well-respected society matron. Not the aristocratic concept of a "good" match, but the pair *had* met in the refreshment line of a ballroom.

Hawkridge's wife was a commoner as well, but an heiress. The ton could overlook almost any sin if the sinner were in possession of a sizable enough fortune.

In Wainwright's case, he and his wife were both highborn. As for Max, he was the disreputable half of his union, but not insurmountably so. The Cloven Hoof did cater to a rougher crowd, but its clientele also boasted a fair number of lords.

Julian was the highest ranking of all five of them. And who was the woman who would not quit his mind? Not an heiress. Not the daughter of a lesser peer. Not even the distant cousin many times removed of a matron of polite society.

Unity Thorne, *courtesan*. Could she be any more beyond the pale?

Julian didn't mind her profession or any other part of her past. That a woman worked as a courtesan or on stage or anything else she needed or chose to do with her life was the woman's business, not his.

But Julian was a duke. His duchess would be the *ton's* business. And they would not be kind.

"She works," he said at last.

Lord Wainwright clasped his hands to his cravat and gasped dramatically.

Max rolled his eyes. "*I* 'work.'"

"My wife is a headmistress," Lord Hawkridge pointed out.

"And mine sold drawings because she didn't have a farthing," Grenville said.

"Once she's betrothed to you, she certainly won't have to *keep* working," Wainwright put in. "Unless her name is on playbills. Is it the sort of employment the ton would hear about?"

Julian swirled his sherry. No, Unity's name would not appear on playbills, despite her presence at the theatre.

And as to her *other* performances... Julian had not heard of her before she appeared on his doorstep, and he'd hosted many fashionable demimondaines at his parties over the years. For better or worse, Unity was not a popular enough courtesan to be recognized by the beau monde.

"They'll know she's different by looking at her," he said tightly. It was unfair that the color of one's skin should signify any more or less than the color of one's eyes or the color of one's hair. "She is of African descent."

"So is Queen Charlotte," Max said without hesitation.

"And people say horrid things about *her*," Julian pointed out.

"And yet she's queen, which is all that matters," Wainwright said. "But it is not so dire. Many Black people have been accepted by polite society, going back decades. Distant royalty is always welcome. In lieu of a title, possessing enough coin would open a few more doors. Is your paramour an heiress?"

"She is not."

"Could you say she was?" the earl suggested. "If no one knows the truth but you, she might seem acceptable to—"

"She *is* acceptable," Julian exploded. "There's nothing wrong with her! Not her trade, not her skin, not her ambition and independence. It is society's rules that are rigid. I don't care if they shun me. More money or a different heritage wouldn't make me like Unity more. If the bucks and the biddies cannot accept her, then I am not interested in pandering to their useless opinions."

All four friends stared at him.

"Er," Wainwright said at last. "Wasn't it *you* that always said you'd one day marry a paragon of society because you'd settle for nothing less than the very best?"

Best. What a stupid, subjective word.

"I do not and will not 'settle' in any aspect of my life." Julian curled his lip. "I am simply saying that Beau Brummell's or the patronesses' idea of 'best' is unlikely to be the same as mine."

"That's very interesting," Hawkridge said. "Given that 'paragon of society' *is* the patronesses idea of 'best.' It sounds like you might have changed your own definition."

"Better yet," said Wainwright, "it sounds like this not-very-paragon might have changed Lambley. Never say you have caught yourself—" He made a dramatic expression. "—*unbending*."

"The gossip would be vicious." Julian's voice was bleak. "They would accuse her of social-climbing and find fault in every word or gesture. I won't have my wife live a life of hurt or fear or slander. Even the title of duchess would not be enough to win a seat at their tables."

Max lifted a sardonic brow. "Does she *want* a seat at those tables?"

Julian stared. Probably not. That was a very good point, but not the only aspect to consider. "My heirs—"

Max's lips quirked.

Julian glared at him. "*What.*"

"*You* aren't part of polite society. Right now. On purpose. What makes you think your children would be happier conforming to 'values' you hate, instead of being who they are?"

Julian set down his empty glass. "I..."

"Maybe they'll never have an Almack's voucher. But they'll still be lords or ladies with all the privilege that offers." Max refilled the sherry. "Didn't we all agree that 'polite society' will overlook anything if one's purse is heavy enough? And aren't you one of the richest peers in all the peerage?"

Julian blinked at him.

"Then it sounds to me," Max continued, "that your children will be fine, and the only opinion you should worry about courting is that of your intended bride. If *she's* willing to put up with the snide comments of a 'polite' society she has no interest in mingling with, then what exactly is standing in your way?"

"You're scandalous…" Hawkridge pointed out helpfully. "She's scandalous… You're both already *not* part of a society that disapproves of *and* disinterests you…"

"I heard him," Julian growled. "I got it the first time."

"Did you?" Grenville asked softly.

"It wouldn't even be breaking new ground," Wainwright put in. "You wouldn't be the first peer to marry his mistress."

"Or even the first duke to do so," Hawkridge agreed. "Lavinia Fenton became the Duchess of Bolton—"

"That was seventy years ago," Julian muttered.

"Common courtesan Sophia Dubochet married Lord Berwick *seven* years ago," Wainwright said. "Is that recent enough for you?"

"He's a baron, not a duke."

"And a third choice at that," Grenville pointed out. "Viscount Deerhurst *and* the Duke of Leinster pursued her first. Surely you cannot question His Grace's pedigree."

"What about Anne Parsons?" Wainwright lifted his sherry. "Lover to the first Prime Minister, the Duke of Grafton. Who she did *not* marry… because she threw him over for the Duke of Dorset, whom she *did* marry."

Max refilled Julian's glass. "You'd actually be the least scandalous of all of them. You're not stealing her from some other duke. There's no eyebrow-raising age difference. No one even knows she *is* your mistress—"

"She is *not* my mistress."

"Then there you go. Your story is embarrassingly boring." Max grinned at him. "What are the gossips supposed to talk about?"

Julian glared at his friends. "You make it sound easy."

"It's not easy," Hawkridge admitted. "They *will* be vicious. She won't be accepted everywhere. Her class, her history, her skin… You're right about all of it. But should that stop you?"

"I would rather have my Nora than the approval of self-important prigs," Grenville said softly. "You have to decide what matters most to *you.*"

There was only one answer to that question.

Julian stared at his glass of sherry then scrubbed his face with his hands. "What's happening to me?"

"Feelings," Max said with pity. "They're the devil."

Julian groaned and pushed away his goblet. They were right. The game wasn't *win the beau monde*. The game was *win Unity*.

He rose to his feet. "I'm leaving before you four squidgy muffins make me any softer."

"Too late," Wainwright whispered to Hawkridge. "Lambley was lovesick before he walked through the door."

Grenville caught up to Julian just outside the Cloven Hoof, before he could reach his carriage.

"I know you told me to stop investigating," he began.

"I meant it," Julian said quickly. "Even if she has dozens of scandalous secrets, she'll tell me when she's ready."

"She might have fewer than you think," Grenville replied. "She's not a courtesan."

Julian stopped walking. "What?"

"Miss Thorne isn't a courtesan," Grenville repeated. "She never was."

She was an *innocent?* Then why did she—

But of course. She had wanted a moment of his time, and he was just as judgmental as the supercilious nobs he disdained, if in a different way. Presenting herself as a courtesan was no doubt how she'd convinced his butler to allow her through the door.

"Find out everything you can about Roger Thorne," Julian commanded. He knew what it was like to have a guardian who only looked after his own interests. This was worse.

A man who tossed his young, penniless

cousin into the gutter was no kind of man at all. Unity hadn't had the legal or financial means to fight back, but Julian was not so limited. Mr. Thorne did not deserve the title of gentleman—or the rewards he'd reaped by exploiting an underage girl with no other options.

Grenville nodded. "I'll report daily."

Julian leapt into his carriage. That was it. No more masks. Unity should not have to be anyone but Unity. There was nothing she needed to prove. Julian liked her exactly as she was.

So what did he plan to do about it?

CHAPTER 18

*U*nity had yearned for Julian all week, but her days and nights had been filled with preparations and rehearsals for the theatre's newest play, which had opened to great acclaim the evening before.

In fact, the success of tonight's performance was why she was late to the masquerade. The actors had taken bow after bow, and Unity's friends had been so bubbly with excitement, they scarcely sat still long enough for her to remove their wigs and prosthetics and cosmetics.

Thanks to the extravagantly generous wages Julian was paying her, Unity no longer needed the meager salary she earned at the theatre. The costumes, however, were invaluable.

The night butler held open the door.

"Cleopatra!" he exclaimed with admiration. "You look absolutely resplendent."

She inclined her head regally. "Thank you, Mr. Fairfax."

It was after midnight. Unity was the last to arrive. The party would be in full swing, every inch overflowing with giddy revelers.

In seconds, she was across the entryway and through the opposite door, bursting into the crowded ballroom to cries of, "Lady X!" amid the music of crystal champagne flutes clinking in toast.

Julian found her at once.

He didn't just lock eyes with her. He parted the crowd with his bold stride, caught her by the waist and pressed her to him, then covered her mouth with his.

She kissed him back, putting six days of longing into the kiss.

His kiss tasted the same way. Desperate, delighted, decadent. Society might not condone intermingling of their worlds, but one could always build a bridge between any two people. She could no more keep herself from his embrace than the sky could ignore the stars.

"I missed you," he growled against her lips.

She fluttered her lashes. "You cannot have been afraid I wouldn't come. I'm still waiting for a proper tour of the abovestairs accommodations."

He gave her a strange look.

Perhaps the eye-fluttering had not been clear. *He* was maskless, as always, but Cleopatra wore a glittering ebony mask framed by white feathers before her eyes.

She looped her arm through his and infused

her voice with a teasing tone. "I'm here. What completely unnecessary and eye-wateringly boring minute change would you like to show off for me today?"

"We shall inspect the perimeter," he informed her and all but dragged her to the closest refreshment table.

Her shortbread had a place of honor atop a multi-tiered silver dessert tray.

Not just her shortbread. Several of the ideas she'd presented to him over the past weeks were on display, here and throughout the ballroom.

She gestured at a new arrangement of armchairs. "You accepted my sketches so begrudgingly, I thought you were 'testing their efficacy' under duress!"

"I was," he agreed shamelessly, his eyes twinkling. "I condescended to conduct the experiments only to prove you wrong."

"But I wasn't wrong?"

"Not always," he said grudgingly.

She pressed a hand to her throat. "Such... high praise. I fear I may faint. The emotion... it's overwhelming."

"If you swoon, I'll catch you," he promised. "I have studied the precise angles and proper stance for maximum efficiency when rescuing overset young ladies."

"I'll bet you have," she said with a laugh. "Go on, show me the rest. Which of my other ideas were slightly less terrible than the ones you came up with?"

But as he led her about the ballroom, pointing out this slight modification and that subtle difference, Unity's eyes were not on the improvements she'd brought about, but rather gazing at Julian's animated countenance.

He was pleased. He was delighted with her. With *them*. No one else understood his obsessions. Not only didn't she think him mad, she matched his meticulousness with her own. She matched *him*.

Her heart filled to bursting. Not out of pride for being useful, but because it was she who had brought these smiles to his infamously hard, intractable face.

She loved him.

It was as simple and as awful as that. He hadn't even ravished her in his sin alcoves upstairs, and she was ruined beyond measure all the same. She wanted to put those smiles on his face forever. She wanted—

"*Unity?*" blurted a disbelieving voice.

She could feel the frost hardening over his good spirits.

"Out," he said in the softest, most terrifying tone she had ever heard.

"It's all right," she said quickly, and took the mortified actress's trembling hand. "*Lady X,* your instincts are correct, but this is not the moment for this discussion."

"I'm so sorry," the theatre's lead soprano babbled, blanching at whatever she saw on the duke's face. "I didn't mean—I just—I—"

"Banned," Julian said coldly. "For life. As are whichever guests brought you. The rules—"

"Stop it," Unity hissed. "It was an accident. Of course she was surprised to discover someone like me as your guest. I don't belong here and we both know it."

"Guest?" he repeated, his tone laced with warning.

She lifted a palm. "Employee? Charity case?"

He dragged her away from the actress, leaving the dumbfounded soprano open-mouthed and pale.

Unity's feet could barely keep up as he parted the crowd and hauled her up the grand marble staircase to the first landing.

"Lords and Ladies X," he called out over the railing. "Are you enjoying the ball?"

Deafening whoops filled the air as champagne glasses shot skyward, clinking and spilling over.

Julian laced his fingers with Unity's and lifted their linked hands high. "You have Lady X to thank for all of the recent improvements."

"Lady X! Lady X!" The crowd was in raptures.

"Leave it to Lambley to poach the prettiest maiden," called a male voice in the back. "I never even got my dance."

The Robin Redbreast. Her cheeks burned.

Julian grinned at her.

"Prettiest and cleverest. I've an entire journal filled with her ideas." He slipped his free hand beneath his lapel and pulled out the second journal Unity had given him. The one where she wrote down all of her ideas for improving his parties.

The revelers cheered as though their duke had produced the holy grail.

Julian held the book aloft. "I have rigorously tested each suggestion and empirically proven them to be sound."

"I thought you said 'some' of them," she whispered.

"A *few* of them," he corrected, his eyes teasing.

Changes that no one in the teeming ball-room was likely to have noticed except for Unity and the Duke of Lambley.

"Kiss her!" yelled another voice.

The crowd whooped its approval.

Julian tucked the journal back inside its nook for safety and cocked an arrogant eyebrow at Unity. "Lady X, who most definitely belongs in this ballroom, may I please have this kiss?"

"I suppose I could test your skills empirically," she returned cheekily.

The revelers roared with laughter. "Test him! Test him!"

Before Julian could move, Unity rose on her toes and kissed him.

She had understood his message. He was giving her the recognition she'd always craved. Not just admitting privately how much he appreciated her, but showing that appreciation to the entire ballroom.

He was sharing not just the credit, but control. Possibly for the first time since inheriting the dukedom. Sharing his *throne*, as though she ruled at his side, as his equal. Her head swam.

Julian wasn't ashamed to have her in his world. He was proud. He was showing her off in front of his peers and hundreds of witnesses. For the first time in *Unity's* life, she wasn't acting behind the scenes.

She was on stage. In the footlights, not hidden behind the curtain. Acknowledged. Valued.

This was her opportunity to make a name for herself in a way that she'd never been offered before. For all these people to know who she was—and to associate her with wonderful masquerades. To look at her golden-brown face and see someone successful, someone who mattered. Someone who was going to achieve her dreams.

"W-would you untie my mask?" she managed to stammer as she stared up at him.

He gave her another kiss. When he pulled away, the ebony mask with the white feathers dangled from his hand.

"Shall I introduce you to my friends?"

She took a deep breath and turned to face the crowd. "I'm ready."

He laced his fingers with hers again. "Lords and Ladies X, the one and only Miss Unity Thorne!"

Fresh bottles of champagne popped in unison from every corner. The crowd's ebullient cheer shook the chandeliers, clinking the crystals together in a dazzling array of light.

Her heart raced wildly and her mouth could not stop smiling.

"What now?" he asked softly. "The night is yours."

She fluttered her lashes, this time knowing he could see them. "Shall we take our private party upstairs?"

"I have a better idea." His voice rasped and his gaze was hot. "Come with me."

CHAPTER 19

They could barely stay out of each other's arms as the duke led Unity up the grand stairs and along the balcony promenade to a nondescript wooden panel.

At Julian's knock, the panel slid open to reveal a hidden doorway leading to the main quarters of his house. Kissing, laughing, they stumbled along the corridor and into an enormous bedchamber dominated by a grand four-poster bed with luxurious deep blue draperies held back against the posts by velvet ropes.

Julian lifted his mouth from hers in order to close and secure the door. When he turned back to Unity, his eyes still sparked with passion, but he did not pull her back into his arms.

"We should talk first."

She stared at him in disbelief, her heart pounding and her mouth still tasting of his kiss. "You brought me up here to *talk*?"

He gestured for her to take a seat in a plushly

upholstered claw-foot armchair beside an equally imposing dressing table.

She folded her arms instead.

"Listen," he began, and then said nothing else. His eyes raked her in obvious hunger, and he visibly forced his hands behind his back as though to prevent himself from reaching for her.

She did her best to glower menacingly at him, the way he always did to others.

He winced and rubbed his face.

"What is the matter?" she burst out. "Listen to what? Are musicians supposed to burst in and surprise us with song?"

"No, I..." He started to step forward, then thought better of it. "Unity, I know you're not a courtesan. You've never traded yourself for coin."

She blinked. "*That's* my crime?"

"It's not a crime. I—"

"Wait." She narrowed her eyes. "How would you know what I choose to do with my body?"

He made a pained expression. "I had you investigated."

"You *what?* To know I've 'never' prostituted myself means you pried into years of my private life, digging for secrets that have nothing to do with you."

"I realize it may sound upsetting—"

"*Do* you?" She could not believe his arrogance and entitlement. "Would it have been acceptable for me to have done the same to you?"

"You don't have to investigate me," he said dryly. "My name is everywhere, whether I like it or not. Debrett's, transcriptions of parliamentary debates, every other scandal sheet..."

"So, because parts of *your* life are public, *I* don't deserve privacy?"

He met her gaze. "I have never misrepresented who and what I am."

"Nor would you have allowed me a moment of your time if I hadn't," she snapped.

"How do you know?" he asked archly. "Did you conduct unauthorized research into what sort of person I might be?"

Unity glared at him.

Oh, very well. She had conducted light "research," insofar as begging gossip from actresses could be counted as a private investigation. She had not knocked on his door unaware of what sort of man he was. And Julian was right—he had made no attempt to hide his true self.

"Why does my history matter?" she asked. "This is a masquerade. We're all in costume as someone else. The whole idea is to remain anonymous, without revealing our true identities."

"I *want* to be with the real you," he replied. "That's why it matters. I can only imagine what you think of me, but I am not a debaucher of virgins. As soon as I realized you were actually an innocent—"

She burst out laughing. "How can you be friends with thousands of people and still not know anything about women? Do you honestly believe the only flavors we come in are 'whore' and 'virgin'?"

"I..." He stared at her in consternation. "Until a young lady is wed, she is typically expected..."

"It wasn't much of an investigation if it didn't turn up the tiny detail that I am not an aristocratic young lady with pretensions to the beau monde," she said dryly. "Your rules are as may be, but you cannot believe the rest of the world abides by them."

He frowned. "You're... not..."

"No, not for a long time. And not sorry about it, either. If you are now bothered by the idea that I am not as 'chaste' as you imagined, may I remind you that none of your many invited guests flood your ballroom on Saturday nights with any expectation of propriety?"

He looked at her in silence.

"They steal away in pairs or more, out to hidden enclaves in the garden, or up the stairs to the private play chambers. With each other, or, often enough, with you. It would be the height of hypocrisy to have a special rulebook that applies only to me. But if the truth has caused you to dislike me—"

"No," he burst out. "That is the point I am trying rather bumblingly to make. I *do* like you. Everything about you. More than I've ever liked anyone. There is only one thing I want more than to be naked in those bedsheets with you, and that is make love as ourselves. Not as strangers with secrets. As Julian and Unity."

She stared at him, speechless, all the fight gone out of her.

"To be clear," she said slowly. "You brought me to this bedchamber out of the express desire to make love to me, regardless of my personal history?"

"To be clear," he answered. "You followed me into this bedchamber out of the express desire for that exact carnal circumstance to transpire?"

"There," she said. "We do understand each other. But in the future, ask me your questions directly. Call off your investigator."

"I already did." He cupped her cheek. "Let us waste no more time on the past or the future and enjoy each other in this moment."

Unity expected him to kiss her, but he waited, letting the choice be hers.

This was The Moment, she realized suddenly. The one and only moment. Of course he had called off his bloodhound. There *was* no future. Once the Duke of Lambley sampled a woman, he never cared to do so again.

After tonight, he would be done with her.

She had never expected anything more. If anything, she was surprised to have kept his interest for as long as she had. The season was coming to a close anyway. His masquerades would end, and they would part ways exactly as they both had planned.

But first, they would share this moment together.

Rather than kiss him, she placed her palms just below his shoulders and pushed him backwards onto the bed.

"What are you doing?" he asked as he elbowed his way up toward the pillows.

"Ravishing you." She hiked her skirts above the knees so she could climb up him and straddle his hips.

"Ravishing... *me*?" He reached for her.

She laced her fingers with his and forced both hands down beside his head. Now she was leaning over him, her bosom brushing against his cravat.

"I suppose you had some notion of 'possessing' me in this bed?"

He licked his lips. "The thought might have crossed my mind."

"I don't want to be your possession." She brushed her mouth against his. "The rest of the world is hard enough. I want equality between you and me, or nothing. Especially in the bedroom."

"Terms accepted." He lifted his head to try and kiss her fully, and this time she let him.

Or rather—she kissed him back. Kissed him *equally*. Passion for passion, kiss for kiss.

Finally, she had him where she wanted him. And oh, how she wanted him. She'd known from her first glimpse of him through his spotless mullioned windows that he would be her ruin. She didn't care. All that mattered was this kiss, this bed, this chance to do what they'd been dancing around from the moment they met.

She untangled her fingers from his and leaned upright to try and unknot his neckcloth. He lifted his hands to do it for her. She pushed his wrists back down onto the pillows and returned her fingers to his cravat.

His arms twitched as though it were physically killing him to keep his hands still rather than try to take control. She kissed him even deeper.

She untied the neckcloth slowly. Learning its folds. Learning *him.*

If they were only to have one night together—perhaps less, perhaps he could only spare an hour—she intended to savor every moment that she could.

When the neckcloth was free, she broke the kiss to toss the square of linen away, then leaned back so that she was fully seated astride him. She unbuttoned his elegant dress coat, tilting her hips to free each side of the coat and push it onto the blanket at his sides.

He lifted his shoulders as though to wriggle out of the garment himself, and she gently pushed him back onto the mattress.

"Am I allowed to do nothing?" he growled.

She smiled at him. "You're going to be allowed to do everything. But you have to wait for it."

He groaned. "I want you now. If you would let me take control—"

She licked the corners of his lips. "Letting someone else hold the reins is the truest test of control. *Self* control."

"I don't have any," he muttered.

But he forced himself to stay in place, watching her with heated eyes.

Was it any wonder she loved him? She dipped her head so that he could not read her expression, and pulled the hem of his shirt from his waistband, pushing the soft cambric up inch by inch, allowing her eyes and her fingertips to learn the hard planes of his abdomen.

When her fingertips reached his nipples, she lowered her head to taste his skin with her tongue.

His stomach tightened, his arms twitching as if desperate to reach for her, but he held his position.

She scooted down, her thighs sliding over his until her mouth was just above his waistband.

"Maybe I should investigate you," she purred.

"Do... whatever you want..."

She unhooked the buttons of his fall and slid her hand beneath to grip him fully. "How many people have you spirited through your secret panel and into this room?"

"None," he gasped. "Until you."

Her breath caught and her heart pounded even faster.

This was his private bedchamber. Not his

salon of sin above the masquerade. This was where he was truly himself. A place where neither of them need hide behind a mask. He brought her here because he wanted to be with *her*. To have a moment that was real.

Unity wanted that, and so much more.

But she would start with this.

She lowered her head and rewarded them both by becoming too occupied to ask more questions.

CHAPTER 20

Julian closed his eyes when she took him into her mouth, then immediately opened them. He didn't want to miss a single moment of making love to Unity.

He knew what would inevitably happen. They would enjoy each other, then go their separate ways. It's what always happened. It was what he preferred, what he had always engineered.

But he didn't want her to walk away. He wanted to keep her.

No—he wanted her to want to keep *him*.

He had never invited anyone into his personal quarters, into his real life. It was terrifying. If this was the end—if, after they found their pleasure with each other, they never found each other again—his private rooms would always remind him of Unity. His bed would forever hold the memory of the time she had been in it with him, of the moments they'd shared in each other's arms.

If she *let* him hold her, that was.

God, he wanted to hold her. To kiss her, to love her, to...

Love.

There was no sense denying it anymore. His heart was perfectly capable of the emotion, and had in fact gone completely off script and tumbled irrevocably in love with the woman who was bringing him perilously close to release.

"Stop," he croaked. "I want... I want..."

"I will give you what you want." She removed her mouth, then licked him from base to tip before lifting her head with a smile. "Or maybe I won't. Are you in control?"

"Yes," he promised. But it was a lie.

She was in control and she knew it.

Julian had never relinquished the upper hand before. Never suspected it could be so erotic.

She slowly kissed her way up his torso. He *could* reach for her. Could toss her onto her back and bury his face between her thighs and show her exactly what he was capable of.

By doing as she asked, by restraining himself, they were *sharing* control.

It was almost as terrifying as being in love.

When at last her lips finally reached his mouth, he kissed her with unrestrained hunger. It was one thing to admit to himself he was in love, despite all his attempts to protect his heart from the vulnerability of such an emotion.

It was another thing to *fight* for love. To prove what was in one's heart to someone else. Through the means of *their* choice. Even if the effort might not work. Even if the uncertainty was killing him.

"May I touch you?" he asked hoarsely.

"Not yet." She lifted her torso.

This time as she straddled him, his breeches were no longer a hindrance, and his cock was free to nudge against the apex of her thighs.

No—he wasn't doing it. She was.

Unity slowly pulled her gown up over her hips, her breasts, her hair, until she wore only her thin chemise. She rocked her hips back and forth against him, rubbing the length of his shaft against her slick heat. Not only pleasuring him, but pleasuring herself.

His fingers gripped the pillows on either side of his head to prevent his arms from reaching for her.

She dropped the gown over the side of the bed with a smile. "Wasn't that easy? Theatre costumes are made to be easily donned and doffed."

What? He didn't care about the costume. He cared about his cock rubbing so deliciously against the place it longed to enter. He cared about the ample hips he yearned to feel beneath his palms. He cared about the dark nipples poking enticingly against her thin chemise. He cared about her soft, delicious mouth too far away to taste.

"May I touch you now?" he begged.

Him, begging. He had never pleaded for anything. But he would beg every night for the rest
of eternity if it led to making love to Unity.

"Not yet." She rubbed herself against him,
slowly, deliberately, torturously. "Patience."

He had no patience. He was drowning.

As she rolled her hips, teasing them both
with the sensual contact, she pulled her chemise
up over her thighs, up over her hips—

Oh god, now he could *see* where their bodies
stroked against each other. His shaft pulsed and
he squeezed his eyes shut against the erotic
sight, only to reopen them immediately there-
after because that fluttery chemise was traveling
up over her breasts and falling to the floor beside the bed.

He never wanted anything more in his life
than to feel those plump breasts in his palms, to
suck those gorgeous brown nipples into his
mouth.

"May I *please* touch you?" He no longer recognized his voice. It was raw, desperation and
desire wrapped together.

She cupped her breasts with her hands. His
groin tightened. After a moment, she reached
down with both hands, pulled his fingers free
from where they gripped each pillow, and
placed his hands on her breasts.

He could barely breathe from the sensation
of finally feeling that soft weight in his palms,
those hard nipples rolling between his fingers.

"See?" she teased breathlessly. "Relinquishing

control does not relinquish your power or your self. You still get what you want in the end. We both do."

"I..." But whatever he was going to say was lost.

Unity was lowering herself onto Julian's shaft. He completely forgot how to speak or breathe or do anything but surge up with his hips in an attempt to penetrate her faster.

She smacked him just above his thigh. "*I* will set the pace."

His cock pulsed in rebellion and delight.

"Did you just... *strike* me?" he gasped.

She grinned. "Did you enjoy it? I can do it again. Harder, if you like."

His bollocks tightened as though they would very much like him to try that one day.

But at this moment, he could think of nothing but Unity. He was finally seated fully within her. She pulled away and then sank back down, slowly, then faster.

As she rode him, she fell forward until her breasts brushed against his cheek, his jaw, his eager mouth. He loved her feel, her taste. She placed his hands on her hips and at last he could grip her tight, feeling the rhythm as her soft curves bounced against him, driving him mad with pleasure.

"Touch me."

Her words were barely a whisper against his hair, but he heard them in his bones. She was close. He could bring her over the edge.

He slid his palm over the softness of her belly, lowering his thumb until it reached the sensitive nub just above where their bodies intertwined. He circled, teased, pinched, stroked, until her muscles tightened and her body shuddered against him, squeezing his shaft with her spasms.

When her orgasm abated, he barely had time to lift her hips from him before spilling his own seed hot across her thigh. Breathing heavily, his heart still galloping, he fumbled for his cravat to clean her skin and then pulled her against his chest, enveloping her in his strong embrace.

Somewhat strong. He was so sated, he could barely move. Or perhaps it was that he did not *wish* to move. Now that he finally had Unity naked and satisfied in his arms, he never wanted to let her go.

CHAPTER 21

Unity had never felt safer and more comfortable than snuggled into the Duke of Lambley's warm, naked embrace.

Part of her still could not believe the man who maintained ruthless control over himself and his surroundings had let her take charge during their lovemaking. From the bewildered expression on his handsome face when they'd begun, it was not something he had ever considered, much less attempted. But he'd done it.

For her.

He was trying to show her that he saw her, that he heard her, that they were equals.

No, that wasn't it either. He had not demanded to take equal control. He had not demanded anything at all. What he was trying to show was that her needs came *first*.

She could have cried from the novelty of it. She hadn't even grasped the enormity as it was happening. And that was it. It was already over.

Any minute now, he would remember his party downstairs, hand Unity her clothes, and walk off to resume his regular life. This moment would not repeat. This embrace would not continue. These arms that were...

Peeling away from her already.

"Unity," he said softly.

She drew herself up stiffly. Their time together had been magical. She would never leave this bed, if it were up to her. But things were no longer up to Unity. The game was over.

It was time to go home.

She slid off of the bed and knelt to rescue her chemise and borrowed gown. It was the last time she'd borrow props from the theatre as well. She wouldn't be back here again. Had no interest in watching Julian escort some other masked vixen up the marble stairs and into the play rooms.

"Unity," he said again. "Look at me."

She pulled on her chemise to give herself time to compose her expression, then turned to him with a mask of peace upon her features.

He had risen up on his elbows, but otherwise had made no effort to cover his gorgeously naked body. How many times had he looked just like this, to someone else? A week from today, would he even remember her name?

"I realize what this is," she said, before he could be the one to tell her. "You don't need me anymore. It's all right. I knew it before we started."

"No." He swung into a sitting position at the edge of the bed, his knees close enough to brush the loose folds of her chemise. "It is you who no longer needs me."

She blinked. "What?"

He visibly took a deep breath. "I investigated you."

"I know," she said. "I told you to stop it."

"I did stop... that investigation," he hedged. "And began a new one into someone else."

His next paramour? She made a face. "What has that to do with me?"

"Roger Thorne is an even worse blackguard than you think he is."

She laughed humorlessly. "I doubt that's possible."

"Unity, *he* was the poor relation. That's why he resented you."

Her lips tightened. "Not the only reason."

"When your parents died, their money was meant for you. As your sole remaining family member, he was its trustee."

Her pulse fluttered. "What are you saying?"

"I'm saying, because the money was not in a trust, he took your rightful inheritance and squandered it, rather than support his ward as an honorable man would have done."

"He spent... *my* money?"

"It's not his club, Unity. It's *your* gentlemen's club. It was built with your money, staffed with your money. You were underage, so he put every penny of your inheritance in his name as quickly as possible."

Her head felt faint.

"*M-my* club?" she stammered. Then the full impact hit her. "My grandfather *didn't* give away the family fortune?"

She had *known* they were wealthy. And then allowed Roger to convince her she'd had a child's understanding of her parents' finances. That the money was unrecoverable. That Unity had not even been mentioned in the will and testament.

All of it, lies.

Julian reached for her hands and cradled them between his knees. "Your inheritance isn't *gone*. It was in the wrong hands. Your father's will left explicit instructions that you were to inherit everything. But because you were so young, the handling of the money fell to your self-serving cousin. As trustee, Roger had full control of the purse strings."

"That craven scoundrel," she whispered. "If I ever lay eyes on his smug, pasty face again..."

"I've addressed the matter for you and taken care of everything," Julian assured her. "The title for the club is now in your name. Or rather, in the name of an account I've had drawn up for you, along with every penny that should have been yours. You can quit your post at the theatre and—"

She jerked her hands from his lap, shaking.

Once again, someone was appointing himself trustee of Unity's life.

"To manipulate my finances so without a single word of discussion is unbelievably high-handed. Or rather, exactly the sort of arrogance I should expect from someone like you. I wanted to forge my future on my own, or at least be involved in the process. I deserve that right. And *you* come along and—"

"If you feel so indebted," he interrupted, "I won't turn down a twenty percent commission in any enterprise you create from this bounty."

"Twenty percent!" she sputtered. "For money that has nothing to do with you!"

"Ah," he said softly. "So it *is* your inheritance, then. Congratulations, Unity. You possess a respectable fortune and your dastardly cousin is beggared once more."

She glared at him in consternation. Of course it was the best news she'd ever heard. But she could not like being left out of the process. Any decision that upended her life ought to be part of a discussion she was privy to.

"I should have told you," Julian said quickly.

"You should not have told me," she said. "You should have *asked* me. You should have respected me enough to sit down and talk to me before taking sweeping action that would affect my life without my knowledge."

"I know," he said. "And I knew it then, too. Or at least, I realized it after I'd already sent my man of business off with no more instruction than, '*Destroy him.*'"

"Then why..."

"I was in too deep. I'd already done the thing that you were going to be rightfully furious about. If it was all going to blow up in my face and cause me to lose you from my life forever, then at least I would leave you in a better position than the penniless one that scoundrel subjected a grieving child to."

She breathed in slowly, then let out the breath. "What did you do?"

"It's in a legal trust," he said. "In your name alone. Along with significant interest, as if it had been invested properly all these years, as ought to have been done." He named an impossible sum.

She narrowed her eyes. "*Your* money?"

"Not a penny of it. It comes from the profits of Mr. Thorne's club, which arguably also should have been your money all along. Your new nest egg is *yours*, Unity. Just as it always was meant to be. This time, safe in a trust."

"Safe from my cousin," she said bitterly. "But what if I marry?"

He shook his head. "No man can ever touch a farthing of your fortune. Not even a husband. You're completely independent and will never be helpless again."

It wasn't a fortune by his standards. Julian probably spent more money on grapes in a year than her parents had ever seen in their lifetimes.

But it was more than enough to start the venture she had dreamed of for so long.

An inheritance her parents had meant for Unity to have all these years.

"What you choose to do next," Julian said, "is completely up to you. Without any financial pressure."

She frowned. "What I choose to do about what?"

He slid off of the bed and onto his knees, once again taking her hands into his.

"I'm sorry, Unity." He kissed her fingers. "I was high-handed and I was arrogant, and probably a host of other adjectives you were too polite to throw in my face. You're right. I was wrong. I am deeply sorry to have broken your trust."

"I didn't want to be saved." Her voice shook. "I wasn't looking for a savior."

"You saved yourself. *Without* me. Despite Roger Thorne. You saved yourself time and again, from the very beginning. You didn't need me then, and you still don't need me now. I can only hope that you might *choose* me."

Her heart beat faster. "What are you saying?"

"I'm saying, that money is yours and always has been. It didn't come from me. It came from your parents. You can do anything you want with it. Just as you can do anything you please with your life." He gazed up at her, his voice soft. "What I'm hoping you might do... is marry me."

The room seemed to tilt.

"I'll not control you," he said quickly. "You can spend your fortune buying your own food and your own clothes and your own chair to sit on, if it makes you happy. Or you can beggar me down to my last guinea. All *I* need is you. You saved *me*."

She stared down at him. "I saved... you?"

"I didn't believe in love. Didn't believe I was worthy of it. Didn't believe I was capable of it. Life was about control, and never forming attachments with anything or anyone." His thumb stroked the back of her hand. "And then came you."

"I thought I was temporary, too," she whispered.

"So did I. That's what I told myself, reminded myself, *warned* myself. But the ice around my heart could no more resist you than the sun. Your warmth melted my defenses. You made me vulnerable. You terrified me. And now I can think of no worse future than one without you in it."

Her hands shook.

He pressed them to his heart. "Meeting you was like finding the lost piece of my soul, when I hadn't realized there was anything missing."

She swallowed hard.

"Marry me, Unity. Please. I beg you." He released her hands. "Or do not. It is your life, and I will never again attempt to inflict my will upon you without your consent. If you do not wish to marry me as eagerly, as desperately, as I wish to marry you, I will not stop you if you choose to go."

She had dreaded the moment in which she had to walk away.

And now she didn't have to.

That was his gift to her: Choice. He was placing *her* in control. Of not just her own life, but their future together.

"I almost forgot the most important bit of all. Good God, my hands are shaking. I haven't said these words in decades, if I ever did back then." His cheeks flushed and he took a deep breath. "I love you, Unity."

She smiled, her eyes stinging. "I know."

He blinked in surprise. "You… knew?"

"You showed me," she said. "Not your interference with my cousin. I mean you and me, right here on this bed. You didn't say the words, but you didn't have to. You told me with your body. You would never have given up control to anyone you didn't love and trust."

"Let me prove how much every night and every tomorrow." He pressed her fingers to his lips without taking his eyes from hers. "Make me the happiest of men. Marry me. Or at least stay, for as long as you like, and I will do my best to make that be forever."

She gazed down into his hazel eyes.

He was right. She didn't have to prove herself. There was nothing left to prove. Unity had already proven herself over and over, time and again. She was fine. She was complete. She was capable. She was enough, with or without him.

The choice was hers.

She cleared her throat. "Are you certain you wouldn't mind if I... oh, say for example... launched competing masquerades?"

He grinned at her. "As long as you don't mind competing against yourself."

She frowned. "What?"

"I don't want to possess you," he said again. "I want the Duke and Duchess of Lambley to be a team. You should do as you please with your money. It's yours. What I want to do with my life is share every part of it with you. This is your home. These are your parties, too."

She eyed him skeptically. "I can change the order of the fruit trays?"

He blanched, but nodded. "I want you to choose me. I want you to *keep* choosing me, every day. Just as I will keep choosing you, over and over again."

She knelt before him and pressed his hands to her rapidly beating heart. "I've been choosing you, day after day. I chose you when you joined me in the market. I chose you when you made ridiculous rules about kissing. I chose you when you fed me grapes I'd never heard of. I chose you when I walked into this room."

His breath shook. "Are you saying..."

"I'm saying I do choose you. I'll keep choosing you. I love you, you high-handed, arrogant sobersides. Yes. I'll marry you."

"But you *were* teasing about altering my perfect fruit trays?" he whispered.

She burst out laughing and wrapped her arms around his neck. "You realize half of society will not condone our union."

He scooped her up. "You do realize I don't give a fig about their opinions."

"You were scandalous long before I met you," she agreed, trailing a finger along his naked shoulder. "So what is it you do care about?"

He tumbled her onto the bed and climbed between her legs, his eyes glinting wickedly. "Let me show you, duchess."

And so he did.

EPILOGUE

*U*nity stood next to a conveniently located table of hopelessly mis-matched hors d'œuvres and watched as costumed guests streamed through the open doors of her masquerade club.

She could not keep her grin from taking over her face.

This was the twenty-eighth time she'd stood near the entrance to glimpse the first arrivals, and each crowd was larger than the one before.

"You did it," her husband whispered into her ear.

Her chest filled with pride and happiness.

This was once Roger's club, though it never should have belonged to him. As an adolescent, when Unity first started making decisions for the club, it had ceased to feel like Roger's even back then. It was *her* efforts that had made it successful, and it was her efforts again that had completely reimagined it into the vibrant, inclusive, non-scandalous masquerade club it was today.

Hers. Her heart fluttered every time she thought the word.

The previous staff had stayed on. The longest employees remembered her and had always thought of Unity as the one in charge during those years. They had no complaint about working for a woman again, and were proud to be part of something new they could all build together.

Unity had rewarded them all with a bonus after opening night, and the way things were going, would soon be able to increase their monthly wages even more.

"I still think you could find a *small* room to dedicate to carnal activities," her husband murmured. "We could christen it ourselves. I've prepared a notebook with helpful sketches of how you and I could entwine our bodies—"

She elbowed him in the ribs, but could not stop her lips from twitching. "Show me your ideas tonight in our bedchamber."

His gaze heated. "I will do my utmost to convince you of their efficacy."

They had married in the church her grandfather had built. The beautiful ceremony was attended by Sampson, Unity's theatre friends, several of Julian's society and not-so-society friends, and anyone with ties to Unity's parents or grandparents. She had felt her ancestors' presence.

Unity had dedicated a large part of her trust to continuing her grandfather's legacy: helping those in their community who had no hope of obtaining help elsewhere. The interest on her loans was shockingly low, as was the barrier to approval. One need only ask and have a worthy cause, and relief would be provided that same day.

One such recipient rushed up to Unity now, unrecognizable in a court jester costume, complete with bells on his upturned toes.

"Thank you again, Your Grace. I'll never forget your kindness."

He was borne off by the crowd before she could do more than smile in return.

Her face was unhidden. Like her husband beside her, she had forborne wearing a mask at a party she was hosting.

Although nothing objectionable took place between the walls of her new assembly rooms, the Duke and Duchess of Lambley would forever remain unapologetically scandalous. They were proud of their union, proud of each other's very different masquerades, and too busy enjoying their lives with each other to care which patroness they'd given a fit of the vapors this week.

She linked her arm through Julian's. The cheerful pomona green of his waistcoat matched the expensive silk of Unity's flowing, lavish ball gown. *Hers*, not borrowed from the theatre. She and Julian had several pairs of subtly coordinating evening attire they wore to their masquerades.

There was no need to dress as a swan or goddess or medieval princess in a tall conical hennin. Unity bubbled over with happiness exactly as she was. In *this* life. With *this* man at her side.

Impulsively, she leaned up on her toes to kiss him.

The gold in his eyes sparkled. "Good heavens, Your Grace. Is this *that* kind of club? People are going to think we're madly in love."

She grinned back at him. "I don't mind if the whole world knows it."

He brushed his thumb across her cheek. "I am so proud of you. I never doubted for even a moment."

"Neither did I," she retorted saucily.

With her first weeks' profit, she had reimbursed him for the cost of investigating Roger—and the threat of social and financial ruin which had spurred him to quickly repay the stolen funds.

It might have been her money all along, but she wouldn't have known about it without Julian's arrogant presumption.

"Even your bad ideas are good ones," she said in mock disgust. "Thank you for highhandedly sending your man of business to meddle into *my* business."

"But that was your fault, too," Julian protested, wide-eyed with innocence. "Normally a proper gentleman such as myself would never have done anything so rude and rash, but you had clearly marked that date as Spontaneity Day on my calendar, and I was all out of options."

She snorted. "Watch yourself. I'll show you something spontaneous later..."

"Is it... letting me rearrange your appallingly unaesthetic sandwich trays?" he whispered. "It is so cruel of you to make me stand here in sight of all those haphazard, asymmetrical—"

She pulled him away. "Come, let us whisk your tender sensibilities far away from such an upsetting sight."

"Finally." He drew her into his embrace and waltzed her onto the dance floor. "I wondered when I would ever have you back in my arms."

"Now." She smiled up at him. "And for the rest of our lives."

The Duke and Duchess of Lambley didn't speak for the next several minutes.

They were too engaged in a scandalously romantic kiss.

~

CAN'T GET ENOUGH DUKES?

Keep turning for a sneak peek of THE DUKE HEIST.

WANT MORE STRONG-WILLED WOMEN?

Try THE PERKS OF LOVING A WALL-FLOWER. Keep turning for an excerpt!

~

THANK YOU

AND SNEAK PEEKS

Start a new series for FREE!

THE WILD WYNCHESTERS

This fun-loving, caper-committing family of tight-knit siblings can't help but find love and adventure. Why seduce a duke the normal way, when you can accidentally kidnap one in an elaborately planned heist?

Grab the first book here:
The Governess Gambit

"Erica Ridley is a delight!"
—Julia Quinn

"Irresistible romance and a family of delightful scoundrels... I want to be a Wynchester!"
—Eloisa James

ROGUES TO RICHES

In the Rogues to Riches historical romance series, Cinderella stories aren't just for princesses…

First book FREE:
Lord of Chance

~

DUKES OF WAR

Roguish peers and dashing war heroes return from battle only to be thrust into the splendor and madness of Regency England.

First book FREE:
The Viscount's Tempting Minx

~

12 DUKES OF CHRISTMAS

Heartwarming Regency romps nestled in a picturesque snow-covered village. After all, nothing heats up a winter night quite like finding oneself in the arms of a duke!

First book FREE:
Once Upon a Duke

~

GOTHIC LOVE STORIES

Prefer atmospheric romance with dark heroes, strong emotion, and an edge of danger?

First book FREE:
Too Wicked to Kiss

Love talking books with fellow readers?

Join the *Historical Romance Book Club* for prizes, books, and live chats with your favorite romance authors:
Facebook.com/groups/HistRomBookClub

And check out the official website for sneak peeks and more:
www.EricaRidley.com/books

THE DUKE HEIST

WILD WYNCHESTERS #1

A secret identities, class divide romance from a *New York Times* bestselling author: Why seduce a duke the normal way, when you can accidentally kidnap one in an elaborately planned heist?

Chloe Wynchester is completely forgettable -- a curse that gives her the ability to blend into any crowd. When the only father she's ever known makes a dying wish for his adopted family of orphans to recover a missing painting, she's the first one her siblings turn to for stealing it back. No one expects that in doing so, she'll also abduct a handsome duke.

Lawrence Gosling, the Duke of Faircliffe, is tortured by his father's mistakes. To repair his estate's ruined reputation, he must wed a highborn heiress. Yet when he finds himself in a carriage being driven hell-for-leather down the cobblestone streets of London by a beautiful woman who refuses to heed his commands, he fears his heart is hers. But how can he sacrifice his family's legacy to follow true love?

"Erica Ridley is a delight!"
　　—Julia Quinn

"Irresistible romance and a family of delightful scoundrels... I want to be a Wynchester!"
　　—Eloisa James

*M*iss Chloe Wynchester folded her hands in her lap and did her best not to glare a hole right through the handsome, haughty Duke of Faircliffe. His frigid blue gaze had looked right at her—and slid away just as quickly, having glimpsed nothing to attract his interest.

How many times had she and Faircliffe been in the same room? Eight? Ten? Every disdainful glance in her direction as indifferent as the last. She lifted her chin. Her father had taught her that to the right person, she would be visible and memorable. Faircliffe was clearly the wrong person.

Not that she *wanted* him to notice her, Chloe reminded herself. The continued success of "Jane Brown" hinged on her uncanny ability to be wholly unremarkable under any circumstances. She gripped the soft muslin of her skirt and took in all the other ladies in the parlor.

Mrs. York clapped her hands together. "And now… a celebratory tea!"

The duke's face displayed a comical look of alarm. "I don't think—"

"You must join us!" Mrs. York's hands flapped like frightened birds. "The girls were about to have oatcakes and cucumber sandwiches before you arrived."

"We were about to discuss epistolary structure in eighteenth-century French novels," Philippa murmured.

"I never meant to interrupt," Faircliffe said with haste. "I mustn't stay, and in fact—"

"Nonsense! Come, come, all of you." Mrs. York waved her arms about the room, driving her guests into the dining room like a shepherd herding sheep.

Chloe and Faircliffe were both caught in the flow.

Once they reached the door, however, Chloe stepped to one side. She could not take a seat at the table, or she would be stuck there for the next hour.

While everyone else was occupied, *this* was her chance to liberate the painting. But first, she needed an excuse to disappear. An adorable, furry reason.

She released Tiglet from the large wicker basket. The calico kitten darted between boots and beneath petticoats with a formidable *rawr.*

Mrs. York gave a dramatic shriek in response.

Tiglet scaled several curtains in search of an open window before darting out of the dining room and flying off down the corridor as though his tail were afire.

Chloe gasped, as if shocked that her homing kitten was attempting to dash home. "How embarrassing! I'll run and find the naughty little scamp at once. Go on ahead. Please don't wait for me."

With her basket hanging from her arm, she ducked into the parlor and closed the door behind her. She hurried to lift the painting from the wall and carried it behind a chinoiserie folding screen in the corner. Up came the frame's grips, off came the backing, out came Bean's painting. She rolled it carefully and tucked it into the basket before stretching the forgery she'd brought over the wooden frame.

She ran to open the parlor door before anyone noticed it had been shut and hurried past the dining room to the front door without taking her leave from the guests. Would anyone notice she failed to return? Doubtful. If anything, the ladies would assume Jane Brown had slunk off in mortification.

Still, there was no time to waste. Any caper's success depended upon a timely exit.

Keeping her head down, she headed down the front walk toward the first carriage in the queue. Only when she glimpsed the red curtains and a pair of leather gloves on the box did she lift her head toward the driver's perch.

It was empty.

Her lungs caught. Where was Graham?

Distant shouts reached her ears, and her tight muscles relaxed. Something unexpected must have occurred, and her siblings' distraction was underway.

This was her cue to flee.

Chloe pushed the basket inside, unhooked the carriage from its post, and leapt onto the coachman's seat. Female drivers weren't unheard of, but all the same, she was glad she never went outside without garbing herself in the plainest, dullest, dowdiest clothes in her wardrobe. No one who glanced her way would bother looking for long.

She set the horses on a swift path out of Mayfair.

Only when Grosvenor Square was no longer visible behind her did she allow herself a small smile of victory.

"Did we escape?" came a low, velvet voice from within the carriage.

Chloe's skin went cold. Who was *that?* Graham wouldn't be hiding in the back of the carriage. A stranger was in the coach! She twisted about and wrenched the privacy curtain to one side.

A handsome visage with soft brown hair and sculpted cheekbones stared back at her, glacial blue eyes wide with surprise.

"*Faircliffe?*" she blurted in disbelief.

"Miss… er… *you?*" he spluttered when he found his voice. "What the devil are you doing driving my carriage?"

Fans of Bridgerton will love this "delightful" Regency romp (Julia Quinn) in which a proper Society miss recruits a very improper lady grifter in a quest for vengeance, and finds love instead.

As a master of disguise, Thomasina Wynchester can be a proper young lady—or a bawdy old man. Anything to solve the case. Her latest assignment unveils a top-secret military cipher covering up an enigma that goes back centuries. But when Tommy's beautiful new client turns out to be the highborn lady she's secretly smitten with, more than the mission is at stake...

Bluestocking Miss Philippa York doesn't believe in love. Her cold heart didn't pitter-patter when she was betrothed to a duke, nor did it break when he married someone else. All Philippa desires is to rescue her priceless manuscript and decode its clues to defeat a powerful enemy. She hates that she needs a man's help—and she's delighted to discover the clever, charming baron at her side is in fact a woman. Her cold heart... did it just pitter-patter?

Get Yours: The Perks of Loving a Wallflower
(Keep turning for a sneak peek!)

Tommy flashed her eyebrows. "Shall we stroll about the room conspicuously?"

"I thought you'd never ask," Philippa whispered.

She rose to her feet, the kitten nestled against her bosom, and made a big show of leading Tommy beneath this ordinary ceiling lunette, then that identical ceiling lunette.

When they reached the farthest point in the room from the chatter of the dining table, Tommy's eyes glittered wickedly and she pitched her voice low. "Alone at last with my fair maiden. Put down the cat so that I can ravish you."

"We're not alone," Philippa said, but her pulse skipped anyway. "There won't be any ravishing."

"Not tonight," Tommy agreed. "Probably. Though I fear it is my sworn duty to change your mind."

"Your sworn duty, or something you *wish* to do?"

Tommy's grin only widened. "Ah. You have seen through me. I wish to ravish you for no other reason than the personal pleasure it would bring both of us."

Philippa's cheeks felt strangely flushed. "You needn't play the rake now, when no one can hear you."

"You can hear me," Tommy said softly.

It was an act. Of course it was an act. But Philippa was reminded of that moment last night in the garden. There had been no music. Just moonlight, and the sound of the wind in the leaves. Tommy had touched Philippa's hip, just as she had when they were waltzing, and for one dizzy moment Philippa had almost thought...

She cleared her throat. "You're incorrigible."

"I've been accused of worse," Tommy replied, and tucked her hands behind her back.

Was it ridiculous to wish that Tommy had not hidden her hands away? That she might touch Philippa again, on the same sensitive spot on her side, just to see whether it would feel like last night all over again, or whether the magic had been a passing fancy?

"I found a letter in my manuscript," Philippa blurted out. Books were a much safer topic.

Tommy gave her all of her attention at once. Or rather, Tommy had already been giving Philippa her full attention, but it sharpened somehow. As though Tommy were a wolf who had just caught the scent of her prey.

"Tell me," she commanded.

Philippa explained her discovery in as condensed a manner as she could manage. How the letter had been hidden, that it had been written by one of the *real* artists of the illuminated manuscript, how all the other copies of the manuscript had been bought up.

"I made a copy of the letter." Philippa turned her back toward the table and pulled the kitten from her chest in order to retrieve a folded square of foolscap.

Tommy's eyes tracked every movement as Philippa's fingers slid beneath her bodice.

"I'm not an artist like Marjorie." Philippa pulled out the copy. "I'm afraid it's just the text in my ordinary handwriting, with none of the flourishes."

"It's perfect." Tommy reached for the folded square and tucked it inside her coat next to her heart. "Graham shall investigate those names at once. Expect an odious amount of detail in an impressively short period of time."

"What if there's no information to find?" Philippa asked. "Whoever they are, Agnes and Katherine need justice, too. Those poor...women..."

Tommy's hand was rising toward Philippa's bodice. Slowly. Affording Philippa time to knock her hand aside or back away. Which she was definitely going to do. Any moment now. Probably.

Before Philippa could make her decision, Tommy's hand passed Philippa's bosom and stopped at her shoulder, where Tommy lifted an errant kitten hair and tossed it aside.

Of course. Of course it was that.

Why would it be anything else? What was Philippa thinking? Was she *not* thinking? All she ever did was think. Why did her best skill fail her so utterly whenever it came to Tommy?

And…what was wrong with Philippa's breathing? Was her bosom heaving? *Was this a heaving bosom?* Even her heart was behaving erratically. What was happening?

Tommy arched a brow as if she sensed Philippa's turmoil and found it amusing. The heavy-lidded expression was similar to the night before, but somehow even more rakish. The slight quirk of Tommy's lips distracted her in a way she had never been distracted before. She should stop staring at Tommy's mouth at once.

Why couldn't she stop staring at Tommy's mouth?

It felt like Tommy was closer than before. Even closer than they had been in the garden, which was ridiculous because she had been *touching* Philippa in the garden, and here they were standing a foot apart. That was why she'd had all the time in the world to notice Tommy's hand rising toward her bosom.

Shoulder. Tommy had plucked cat hair from Philippa's *shoulder*.

There was nothing less sensual than that.

And yet it had felt as though the light touch were a mere precursor, a hint of something bigger, better. An appetizer before the main course.

Mayhap that was why Philippa was still staring at Tommy's parted lips. Even though the moment had stretched on far beyond what was acceptable or explainable.

She wanted Tommy to do it again; to touch her hip, to pluck cat hair from her bosom. She wanted to know if this electricity crackling between them was all in Philippa's head, or if it was as real as a lightning storm, filling the night with white-hot bursts of power and danger.

Tommy's fingers moved. On the side hidden from Mother's guests.

The slender hand was coming not toward her bodice, or even her side, but just enough forward for Tommy to brush her fingertips up the back of Philippa's hand, from her knuckles to her wrist.

She felt the caress all the way to her toes. In places that weren't even her toes. Every inch of her body seemed alive to the possibility of Tommy's touch…and her cold dead heart gave its first unmistakable flutter. Several flutters. Possible apoplexy.

"Philippa!" Mother called.

"Coming," Philippa replied breathlessly.

She did not move. If Tommy had touched her like this last night in the garden, Philippa might have thought she meant to kiss her.

And if that charged moment had felt any-thing like this one…

Philippa would have wanted it to happen.

~

ABOUT THE AUTHOR

Erica Ridley is a *New York Times* and *USA Today* best-selling author of witty, feel-good historical romance novels, including THE DUKE HEIST, featuring the Wild Wynchesters. Why seduce a duke the normal way, when you can accidentally kidnap one in an elaborately planned heist?

In the *12 Dukes of Christmas* series, enjoy witty, heartwarming Regency romps nestled in a picturesque snow-covered village. After all, nothing heats up a winter night quite like finding oneself in the arms of a duke!

Two popular series, the *Dukes of War* and *Rogues to Riches*, feature roguish peers and dashing war heroes who find love amongst the splendor and madness of Regency England.

When not reading or writing romances, Erica can be found riding camels in Africa, zip-lining through rainforests in Central America, or getting hopelessly lost in the middle of Budapest.

~

Let's be friends! Find Erica on:
www.EricaRidley.com

www.ingramcontent.com/pod-product-compliance
Lightning Source LLC
Chambersburg PA
CBHW050810190726
48285CB00005B/1860